SEALED
with a Kiss

AN ALPHA SEALS NOVEL

Makenna Jameison

Copyright © 2015 by Makenna Jameison

ISBN: 9781717898302

ALSO BY MAKENNA JAMEISON

ALPHA SEALS

SEAL the Deal
SEALED with a Kiss
A SEAL's Surrender
A SEAL's Seduction
The SEAL Next Door
Protected by a SEAL
Loved by a SEAL
Tempted by a SEAL
Married to a SEAL

SOLDIER SERIES

Christmas with a Soldier
Valentine from a Soldier
In the Arms of a Soldier
Return of a Soldier
Summer with a Soldier

Table of Contents

Chapter 1

Evan "Flip" Jenkins took a long pull from his bottle of beer, watching the strawberry blonde woman standing near the cooler, chatting with Evan's SEAL team member Patrick "Ice" Foster and Patrick's girlfriend, Rebecca. The woman's long hair gleamed in the sunlight, framing the delicate features of her porcelain skin and emerald green eyes. She burst out laughing, flashing a huge smile that lit up her entire face. Evan wished he was standing closer so he could've heard what made her laugh like that. What he wouldn't do to hear that sound again and again. It was light and carefree, sweet, and feminine. It filled his chest with a stirring he couldn't even begin to describe and seeped deep inside him, lighting his entire body with awareness and desire.

Her snug tank top highlighted her gorgeous curves, the swell of her breasts giving way to a small waist and slender hips. She wore a loose, long skirt beneath it—the swish of it against those silky legs as she walked around earlier had nearly killed him. How he longed to see exactly what was beneath it, the peeks of flesh he'd gotten taunting and teasing him with every delicate step she took. Her feet just barely peeked out beneath the bottom of it, and he saw a hint of dainty sandals and pink toenails. She was so sweet and feminine it practically hurt just to look at her.

A flush spread over her cheeks, probably from the summer heat, but Evan imagined she might look like that after a very thorough kissing from him, in which his hands skimmed over all those supple womanly curves and his mouth claimed hers. An even better image popped into his mind—the woman, crying out in pleasure from beneath his large frame after he'd thrust into her, making her come in his bed. The first of many times he'd pleasure her again and again.

"Man, you've got it bad…," his fellow SEAL Matthew "Gator" Murphy taunted, following Evan's gaze across the backyard.

"How do you figure?" Evan asked, his eyes not leaving the gorgeous redhead.

"You've been staring at her all night, and she hasn't glanced your way once. You're totally fucked."

Evan guffawed, spitting out his beer.

Matthew slapped him on the back and laughed. "Yep, just like I said. Totally fucked."

Evan bit out a curse and turned away, Matthew still chuckling in the background. As the youngest man on his SEAL team, Evan was used to the other guys ribbing him. Still, at twenty-seven, he wasn't exactly some kid fresh out of BUD/S. He'd joined the Navy right out of high school and had proudly served his country for the past nine years. He'd seen more life and death than most guys his age, and he'd accomplished more in his short career than some men could hope to achieve in their entire lives.

Although that earned him respect in other areas of his life, namely where civilians and women were concerned, the other men on his SEAL team still enjoyed giving him a hard time. Especially when it came to women. Those guys were like five big brothers—rough and tumble alpha males, like him, who fought hard and played harder and were fiercely protective of those they cared about. Their unbreakable bond had been tightly forged after years of training together in grueling situations on and off shore and repeated deployments to critical situations all over the world. They were ready to go at a moment's notice and fought swiftly as one unit, gauging each other's reactions and reading one another's thoughts as though their ties had been those of blood brothers.

Not that any of that mattered tonight, judging from the way the other guys were giving him shit over failing to impress a woman.

Hell.

Their team leader, Patrick, had invited the SEALs and their CO over for a barbeque at his place. Some mishap had prevented the CO from hosting it at his home, but Patrick didn't seem too put out by the change in plans. He'd been manning the grill throughout the evening while Rebecca directed guests to the beers in the coolers and food spread out on the table. And his often cold-as-ice team leader had never looked happier.

Hell, if Evan had a home of his own and a woman

at his side, he'd be glad to host shit like this, too. Especially on a balmy summer evening like tonight. The air was warm with just a bit of the salty breeze from the ocean, the scent of the charcoal was mixing in with the delicious aroma of the food on the grill, and he was feeling a bit restless.

If he had a gorgeous lady in his life, he'd be able to enjoy burgers and beers with his buddies and then haul his woman off to bed when the evening was over, ravishing her until morning. Until they were both boneless with exhaustion and thoroughly sated.

Not gonna happen tonight.

The one-night-stands he'd enjoyed over the past few years—hell, the ones he'd enjoyed ever since he'd joined the military—just weren't cutting it anymore. He'd been too old for that kind of thing for a long time now. Sure, he enjoyed female company and the immediate sexual gratification that came from bedding a woman, but afterward? He'd be alone in his apartment night after night, waking up at the ass crack of dawn for PT and drills with no one to come home to at night.

Then he'd meet another woman the following weekend and repeat the cycle again. Ad nauseam.

The redhead his eyes had been glued on all night he'd seen before. He'd briefly met her in passing one day at Rebecca's a month or so ago. Somehow he'd gotten roped into dropping some shit off for Patrick, and she'd been heading out the door just as he got there. Cute little shorts, another tight tank top…hair pulled back in some kind of messy twist that looked cuter than hell on her. She'd grinned up at him, those big green eyes capturing his heart, and hurried off before he'd known what had hit him.

Damn if she wasn't even sexier tonight. Her skirt wasn't revealing like those shorts had been. It was sexier than hell though. Then there was the way all that strawberry blonde hair cascaded around her shoulders. It caressed her breasts as she'd walked around the backyard, enrapturing him. He wondered what all that long, silky hair would feel like whispering across his chest as she rode him. He'd twist his fingers through it, lost in her. Pump into her until she flushed and came for him.

Hell. He'd barely even spoken to her and was already imagining night after night of her in his bed.

He stalked toward the picnic table, which was currently overflowing with platters of food. Ribs, hot dogs, sausages, burgers—just about anything a man could want to chow down on. Patrick had obviously been in charge of the food. No doubt if Rebecca had selected the menu they'd be eating healthy grilled chicken and fish. Maybe those tiny little sandwiches women served at parties.

He grabbed a burger and side of ribs, scooping some potato salad onto his plate and finally adding a hot dog as well for good measure. If only catching the attention of that elusive redhead—Alison—was as easy as grabbing what he wanted for dinner. When they'd been introduced earlier, he'd tried to charm her with a little flirting. She'd politely shaken his hand, flashed him the sweetest smile he'd ever seen, and then breezed right by him, her eyes set on another member of his SEAL team.

It didn't help that when the guys had introduced him they'd pointed out he was the youngest of the men. Save for Patrick, they were all single, and eager for the attention of a gorgeous woman like Alison.

Her eyes had lit up at the amount of testosterone filling the backyard as she scanned the crowd, and before he could even attempt to get to know her, she'd chased after some other guy.

She was barely a few years older than him, if that. Hell, at six-foot-two, he towered above her small frame by a foot. She was slender and petite, with a personality radiating warmth. He was tall with the build of a SEAL, of a man who spent hours doing PT and who had been hardened by war. He always treated women with respect but was used to commanding the attention of a room and getting the woman he chose.

With their testosterone-driven group, the women had always flocked to them. When the guys went out to Anchors, a popular bar near their base in Little Creek, Virginia, they'd practically be fighting the women off. If she thought a younger man couldn't provide for her, care for and pleasure her, she was dead wrong. He'd be more than happy to show her exactly all the ways he wished they were acquainted.

Balancing his plate of food in one hand, he grabbed another beer. His eyes scanned over the crowd, searching. Plotting. He was determined to find a way to catch her eye, and the night was still young.

Mission on.

Chapter 2

Alison excused herself from chatting with Rebecca and Patrick and wandered over to grab something to eat, the rumbling in her stomach reminding her that she needed some sustenance. Since Patrick had immediately pulled her best friend into his muscular arms the moment Alison had stepped away, she didn't think either of them would miss her too much. She was overjoyed to finally see Rebecca so happy after losing her husband a year ago in a terrible car accident. But now that Rebecca was dating a handsome SEAL who seemed completely smitten with her, Alison realized just how lonely she'd become these past few months.

She tossed her empty beer bottle into the recycling bin, listening as it clanked against the others. The barbeque had only started an hour ago, but the hungry men had already put away enough food and drink to feed her for an entire year. If that's what it took for them to keep up with the grueling workouts that got them those strapping muscles and chiseled physiques, she'd take it. And gladly offer to cook for them anytime.

Those guys were a feast for the eyes, and there were several moments tonight where she had to practically stop herself from drooling as she caught sight of one gorgeous man after another.

This was *sooo* not what she needed right now.

Patrick was the one hosting the barbeque tonight. Six insanely hot members of his SEAL team, their CO—who was handsome, too, for a slightly older man—and some guys from base had come over to enjoy a little food and camaraderie. The backyard was now packed with buff military men and their wives or dates. According to Rebecca, all of the other guys on Patrick's team were single, or at least without a serious girlfriend.

Having experienced a recent dating drought with the lack of eligible men in the Virginia Beach area, Alison had been more than happy to join her best friend in hopes of scoping out an unattached SEAL. The last guy she'd dated had been a buttoned-up accountant, and he couldn't have been further from these guys if he'd tried. He was smart and polite, but there was absolutely no spark between them. After two mediocre dates, she'd bid him farewell. Wanting someone serious to settle down with and wanting at least *some* mutual attraction between them wasn't too much to ask, was it? The guy would make a great friend, but sadly, the physical attraction had been strictly one-sided.

She stepped up to the buffet table, watching a young guy pile his plate high with food. He was as big and muscular as the rest of them, but cute rather than devastatingly handsome, with dark blond hair and a baby face. She smiled, thinking he most definitely wouldn't like being told that. His eyes had flashed in warning earlier when another guy—Christopher, was it?—had told her he was the baby of their SEAL team.

The other men had laughed, ribbing him like older brothers, but this guy's eyes had blazed. If she hadn't known better, she'd have thought she sensed a hint of embarrassment there as well. It couldn't be easy competing for women when you were constantly around five other aggressive, assertive alpha males. He probably attracted his fair share of the younger college girls though.

Having just reached the big three-oh, Alison's biological clock was ticking away. She spent her days caring for kids at the hospital as a pediatric nurse and spent many weekends with Rebecca and her daughter, Abby, but it wasn't the same as having kids of her own. Or a house and a husband to take care of her. Not that she needed "taking care of." She had a successful career, plenty of friends, and a great townhouse by the beach.

That didn't stop her from wanting that white picket fence, two point five kids, dog, and a husband.

This guy certainly wasn't looking to settle down. He was big but looked only twenty-five or so, and she didn't date younger men. She'd made that mistake once and had her heart broken when she realized they were at completely different stages of their lives. She'd wanted to get married; he'd wanted to take off for a year to see the world. And he hadn't expected her to wait around for him.

That relationship had ended two years ago, and her heart still hurt if she thought too much about it. No, she'd definitely scope out an older guy this time.

The accountant she'd just met had nearly fit the bill—he was thirty-four, owned a home, had a successful career, and wanted to settle down with a family. Unfortunately, when he'd kissed her goodnight, it had been about as exciting as kissing her brother.

She grabbed a plate and scanned the selection of food.

"Alison, right?" the cute SEAL at the buffet table asked. A grin spread across his tanned face, his blue eyes bright as he gazed down at her. The short buzz-cut of his blond hair screamed military, but something about him was friendly and approachable. Pretty much the opposite of Patrick and some of the other guys.

The rumble of his deep voice caused something to stir inside her, and if he'd been a few years older, losing some of that sweet baby face and looking a little more worldly, she'd probably be melting into a puddle right in front of him.

He must've been at least six feet two inches—her little brother was about his age and height, but not nearly as muscular. This guy's biceps flexed as he reached out to shake her hand. She stared a beat too long, fascinated by his bulging arms. He easily balanced his overflowing plate in his other large hand, and she shook his extended hand, shocked by his warm, sure grip.

"Yes. And you're…?" Her voice trailed off. She knew that she'd met him earlier, but after being introduced to so many members of Patrick's SEAL team, she was having trouble keeping all of their names straight. Not to mention the crazy nicknames each guy also seemed to have. Luckily they addressed one another by their given names in crowds like this.

"Evan Jenkins," he said, his turquoise eyes gleaming with interest. His dark blond lashes framed them perfectly, making him far more attractive than any man had a right to be. This guy must be a real heartbreaker with all the young college girls in this town.

"Right, Evan, sorry. It's tough keeping all the names straight."

"No problem," he said, flashing her an easy grin. His full male lips looked entirely too kissable for her liking. Just a second ago she was thinking he reminded her of her little brother—now she was wondering what it would be like to kiss him? She discreetly shook her head and grabbed some utensils and a napkin.

"I saw you a few weeks ago at Rebecca's," she commented.

"I remember. You were wearing those cute little red shorts."

She cocked her head at him, a blush spreading across her face. "You remember what I was wearing?" That day she'd bumped into him had been ages ago. Still, she had to admit she was a tiny bit flattered this guy would remember what she had on the first time they met.

"Why wouldn't I remember a gorgeous woman like you?" His voice was low, gruff, but there was still a hint of humor in the way he said it.

"I'm sure you guys all meet your fair share of women," she said lightly, maneuvering around him.

He turned to watch her rather than walking away with his already overflowing plate of food.

"Don't worry, I left a few things for you," he joked.

"Not much from the looks of it." She winked and appreciated the broad grin that stretched across his face.

"You're a tiny little thing; how much could you possibly eat?" he laughed.

"More than you think; I've got two younger brothers. I had to make sure to keep up. There wasn't much worse than having two teenage boys in the house when I was growing up." She grabbed a hotdog and put some fruit salad on her plate.

"That's it? Tell you what, I'll let you wrestle me to the ground, and then you can have my plate."

"You'll *let* me? I can think of a few things that could bring you to your knees, but that's not going to happen."

Evan stepped closer, heat flaring in his eyes. She inhaled his clean, masculine scent, surprised at the way her blood pressure rose at his nearness. He brushed back a strand of hair that had blown across her face, and she had to force herself to remain still and not lean into his touch. No matter what she'd decided earlier about him being too young, she had to admit that it felt pretty darn good having his large hand brushing against her skin. She could think of a few places she wouldn't mind feeling his gentle touch. And the desire in his eyes was evidence enough that he would be happy to acquiesce.

Not that she'd allow anything to happen. She was far past the age of making out with the cute guy she'd met at a party. Especially when it would lead nowhere.

"Tell me more about it," he murmured, ducking low so that his lips were at her ear.

"About what?" she asked, momentarily stunned by his closeness.

"That part about you bringing me to my knees," he whispered huskily.

A beat passed, and she almost suggested they get out of there together. As if she was the type of woman who did that sort of thing. Something about this guy had heat and awareness licking through her, her body entirely too responsive to him. He surprised her, intrigued her, even though he was exactly the opposite of her type. Too young. Too macho. Too all wrong for her.

For a flash, she imagined what it would feel like to have him haul her into his arms, to feel those hot lips and hard muscles moving against her.

There was no doubt he'd be up for a good time, but that didn't mean they should actually do anything about it. Guys like him were all about having as many women as they could. She was too old to fall for that game and not at all interested in being added to what was likely a very long list of one-night-stands.

Alison laughed and pulled back, patting him gently on the arm. "Not going to happen, sweetie. I'm way too old for you."

She turned and walked back across the lawn, leaving Evan standing at the table right where she'd found him, looking completely bewildered.

Chapter 3

Evan bit out a curse, watching the supple redhead walk away. No, *walk* was too mild of a description for her movements. She *sashayed* away from him, swinging her hips in that damn skirt as if she knew his eyes would be on her the entire way. It skimmed the curve of her tight ass, sending flames licking through his body and blood rushing to his groin.

Once again, he got a few peeks of her toned legs as she moved, and he longed to feel them tangled between his own. Or better yet, tossed up over his shoulders as he bent down to pleasure her, driving her wild with desire. The need to have her grew stronger with each step she took away from him.

She was feisty, he'd give her that. There was the tiniest dash of spice mixed in with all that sweetness. He was pretty sure his eyes had just about bugged out of his head when she'd mentioned bringing him to his knees. The thought of her taking his throbbing cock into her luscious mouth had made him instantly hard. Thank God he was wearing loose-fitting cargo shorts—truth be told, they'd gotten uncomfortably tight at the moment.

She'd been flirting with him, glancing up beneath those long lashes of hers. He loved that she barely reached his shoulders and had to tilt her head far back to meet his gaze. She was so small, it would take barely any effort at all to lift her into his arms and whisk her away. She'd seemed intrigued for just a second when he'd bent toward her, only to dismiss him a moment later, claiming he was too young for her. Hell if he didn't want to show her all the ways he was not, in fact, *too young*. He was a man, and he certainly knew how to satisfy a woman.

Maybe she was one of those chicks that dug the thrill of the chase. She'd shamelessly flirt with him, but he'd have to do a whole lot of chasing to catch her. He'd enjoyed chasing after women in his younger days, the college girls steadily coming in and out of his apartment every week—and coming in his bed, too, he thought with a wicked grin.

Those types of chicks weren't ready to settle down though—they wanted a good time, the allure of dating an older man, the thrill of being with a Navy SEAL. How ironic that after dating a string of girls who thought of him that way, he was now attracted to a woman who seemed to think he was far too young. Maybe that's what he deserved after chasing after the college co-eds for so long. Wasn't karma a bitch?

He stalked over to the picnic table, grabbing a seat with Christopher "Blade" Walters, Christopher's date, and Matthew. "Struck out again, huh?" Matthew asked sympathetically.

"I don't understand women," he grumbled.

The brunette seated beside Christopher laughed. "Don't worry; we don't understand men either."

"What happened?" Christopher asked.

"The bases were loaded; I was ready to end the night with a home run—"

"And game over," Matthew finished.

"Pretty much, bro," Evan said, biting into his burger. It was damn good, and a helluva lot better than the MREs they'd eaten last week while deployed on a quick mission. He'd grill every night if he had a sweet backyard like this, but his apartment building didn't allow residents to keep grills on their balconies. After wolfing it down, he took on the hot dog, polishing it off in just a few bites. At the moment he was starved for much more than food, but this would have to do. A cold beer chased down the meal but didn't quite alleviate the emptiness he was feeling. What the fuck had gotten into him?

Alison's laughter trailed across the lawn, and he saw her talking with his teammate Brent "Cobra" Rollins. Shit. That guy seemed to draw the ladies to him like moths to a flame. No woman could resist Brent. His bad boy persona seemed to attract all the ladies within a mile radius. Maybe more. It figured he'd set his sights on the one woman Evan was interested in. He didn't really see Alison as Brent's type, but the woman was gorgeous. Even if Brent wasn't interested in a long-term thing with her, he'd humor her, take her out—take her to bed.

The thought of Brent's lips on Alison, of Brent kissing her, making love to her, made his blood boil. No way in hell was he allowing that to happen. If he saw her leaving with Brent, he'd haul her over his shoulder and out the front door—consequences be damned. It had been a long time since a woman had genuinely captured his interest, and he sure wasn't about to let this one slip through his fingers.

He planned to have her one way or another—she just didn't realize it yet.

As he scanned the rest of the yard, he nodded in greeting to Mike "Patch" Hunter, the remaining member of their SEAL team. He was chatting up a pretty lady as well, but Evan couldn't care less about that. His eyes shot daggers at Brent again as Christopher and Matthew chuckled beside him.

"You up for Anchors tomorrow night?" Matthew asked.

"Sure, why the hell not." It's not like he had anything else to do. The thought of sex with some anonymous woman didn't sound quite as enticing as it had in the past though. Flirt, take a woman home, make her breakfast, send her on her way. That routine was getting old.

His eyes flicked back to Alison, and he saw her looking uncertainly around. Brent was nowhere to be seen, and Evan's insides warmed at the thought. Had he shot her down? She seemed way too sweet for him, but then again, he barely knew the first thing about her.

Evan usually was pretty good at reading people— all the guys on the team had to be given the dangerous situations they found themselves in. An error in judgment could mean the difference between life and death in battle, and their skills had been honed over years of experience. He didn't think he was wrong about the vibe he'd gotten from her. She may like to flirt and had enjoyed getting him wound up earlier, but she was sweet and innocent just the same. Definitely not the woman for a commanding, arrogant SEAL like Brent.

His heart wrenched at the slightly lost look in her eyes, but a moment later she was chatting with her friend Rebecca again. Evan sighed. He could relate just a little too closely to the look of longing written all over her face. Just like Alison, he wanted what he couldn't have.

***

Alison hugged Rebecca goodbye and said goodnight to both her and Patrick. The barbeque tonight had been just what she needed. After three grueling twelve-hour shifts at the hospital, she now had a few days off to recuperate. She'd had a great day at the beach and the barbeque, and she was looking forward to a few more days of pool time in her townhouse complex and perhaps another jaunt down to the ocean. Her four days off in a row felt more like a mini vacation in the summer with the water beckoning her, warm sunny days, and barbeques with friends. Alison welcomed the respite.

She walked down the driveway and strode down the sidewalk, listening to the hints of conversations around her. It was after ten, but there were plenty of people around. Others were leaving the party, talking and laughing quietly so as not to disturb the rest of the neighborhood. She passed a couple walking their dog and another guy out for a late jog. It seemed crazy to run this late at night, but she understood wanting to avoid the summer heat. If she were the type of person that enjoyed jogging, she'd probably do it after the sun had gone down, too. The blazing summer days were meant to be spent at the pool or beach, not sweating as you pounded the pavement.

The warm, salty air shifted around her as she walked, and she was glad the weather had been nice for the party. The spacious backyard was the perfect setting for all the guests—she couldn't imagine all those huge military guys cramming into Patrick's house. They'd have been elbow-to-elbow as they stood around his living room.

A gust of wind picked up, and she wrapped her arms around herself as she hurried along. It felt like a storm was blowing in from the ocean. Too bad she hadn't found a closer parking spot, but another minute, and she'd be safe in her car. A bolt of lightning lit up the sky in the distance, and she grumbled to herself as she picked up the pace.

Alison stopped when she got to the crossroad she'd parked on, puzzled. She looked left and right, wondering if she'd somehow gotten turned around and headed in the wrong direction. It was the first time she'd been to Patrick's house, but she'd parked along the main road right beside his neighborhood. It's not like she'd parked blocks away on some side street and was unable to find her way back. This road intersected right with Patrick's street. It didn't get much more straightforward than that.

She scanned back and forth one more time, her heart palpitating. Her car was nowhere in sight.

Several fat drops of rain began falling from the sky, and she cursed. She'd have to go back to Patrick's and hope Rebecca was staying there for the night. Or else ask Patrick if she could wait at his house while she called a cab. He had a young son that was sound asleep, so it's not like he could very easily give her a ride home. She didn't doubt that he would, but waking up a sleeping child to bring them out in this weather seemed like a bad idea.

Wrapping her arms around herself as the rain began to steadily patter down, she turned back toward Patrick's street. She scanned the cars leaving, hoping by some miracle that Rebecca wasn't staying the night and would drive by and give her a lift. A steady stream of headlights filled the street as cars made their way out of the neighborhood, but as she suspected, Rebecca's car was nowhere in sight.

She bit her lip, trying to decide what to do. It looked like hurrying back to Patrick's house was about the only option. She took a few steps forward, looking down to keep the rain off her face.

A moment later, a large black SUV pulled up beside her, and she was relieved to see Evan, the young guy from earlier, unrolling the window.

"Are you okay?" he asked, concern tingeing his voice.

"My car's gone!"

"Get in," he said, leaning over to open the passenger door for her. She gratefully climbed in just as the rain began to heavily fall. Evan switched the wiper blades to the highest speed as the skies opened, and she wiped the droplets of water from her arms, rubbing her damp palms against her long skirt. She was thankful he'd pulled up at that moment; otherwise she'd be soaked through.

"Looks like I got here in the nick of time."

Alison laughed in relief. "That you did. Isn't that what you SEAL types do? Rescue people?"

"SEAL types?" Evan asked with a chuckle.

"You know what I mean."

Evan grinned at her from across the console. "At your service, ma'am."

"Ugh—do not call me ma'am. That makes me think you're talking to my mother."

Evan raised his eyebrows. "Whatever you say, baby."

He winked, and Alison felt a flush creeping across her skin at the way his low, masculine voice uttered the word "baby." She was thankful for the dark interior so that Evan couldn't see just how red her face was. She liked the way he called her that a little *too* much.

"Did you park on this street?" he asked, cocking his head as he watched her. His eyes flashed with interest for a split second before returning back to normal.

"Yeah, Patrick's street was pretty full by the time I arrived. I circled back around and parked right over there." She pointed, which was pretty useless, since there wasn't a car parked on the road anywhere and they couldn't see a thing in the pounding rain.

"It's a hurricane evacuation route," Evan said.

"But we're not in the middle of a hurricane…."

He shrugged, a cocky grin on his face as he gazed over at her. "Probably some overzealous tow truck driver. I'll take you to get your car."

"Thanks, I'd appreciate it. I was getting ready to go find Rebecca to see if she could give me a lift."

"It's no problem."

She shivered as the AC blast over her damp skin. She felt her nipples hardening and hoped Evan wouldn't notice in the dark. She was wearing a flimsy tank top, which was welcome in the oppressive summer heat but not so great in the arctic interior of Evan's SUV. His eyes skimmed over her, and he turned down the air conditioning without comment.

The rain battered against the car as Evan slowly made a U-turn and headed back out the main road. "Don't feel too bad—Brent got his car towed a few months ago from the same spot."

"Seriously? Did they charge him to get it?"

Evan chuckled. "No, Brent can be a scary guy." He cleared his throat, seeming somewhat uncomfortable. Not entirely sure what that was about, Alison pressed him for more information.

"So what'd he do? Some kind of top secret SEAL move on the poor cashier running the impound lot?"

Evan's booming laugh filled the interior. "Something like that."

They came to a stoplight, and Evan glanced her way, raising his eyebrows. "Are you planning a similar strategy? I can be your back-up," he added with a wink.

Alison grinned. "You don't think they'd be intimidated enough by me?"

"If they were smart they would be. It's never a good idea to mess with an angry woman."

"Smart man."

"It's their mistake though—there's no reason for you to pay for a tow when you were parked on a public street."

He pulled forward again as the light turned green, going slowly to work his way through all the standing water on the road. Maybe it was for the best her car had been towed—her little Accord didn't have as much a chance in all this water as Evan's monstrous SUV.

A boom of thunder sounded, and Alison jumped. Evan reached over and gave her arm a reassuring squeeze, his eyes still on the road. "It's okay; you're safe with me."

His words washed over her, comforting her like a warm blanket. Or maybe that was just the burning feeling of his large hand on her arm. She liked the feel of his fingers on her skin a little too much. Even after he removed it, she felt the heat of it there, like he'd imprinted his handprint on her arm. Awareness washed over her at his solid presence at her side. This guy was way too young for her, although she had to admit, she liked how confidently he navigated the flooded streets. How he reassured her when he really had no need. She'd seen that protective instinct in Patrick when he was around Rebecca and her daughter, and Alison realized that all the guys on his SEAL team were that way—alpha males set on controlling the situation and protecting those around them.

"I guess this weather is nothing for you," she commented.

"How's that?"

"Rebecca said you guys train in all kinds of crazy weather. She wasn't too thrilled when Patrick went scuba diving in the middle of a storm."

"True enough. We have to be prepared for anything. I don't have anyone worrying about me at home though like Patrick does."

Alison felt her heart constrict a little. He sounded almost sad, which was crazy, because a young guy like Evan couldn't be looking to settle down. He probably went out with the rest of the guys every week hoping to pick up women. Rebecca had said some of the guys on Patrick's SEAL team seemed to have a new lady with them each time she saw them. Patrick was one of the older guys on the team and had a son, but as for the rest of them? Carousing for ladies seemed to be part of their weekly fun when they were stateside.

She and Rebecca had gone to Anchors a few times years ago. It was popular with the military guys and single women in Virginia Beach, and even when she'd gone it had been more for the experience than the hopes of meeting a great guy. It was a pick-up joint, perfect for checking out the opposite sex and snagging a one-night-stand but not exactly the type of place where you'd go looking for the love of your life. The fact that the rest of Patrick's SEAL team frequented it just further proved her point—if she was looking to settle down in the near future, Evan certainly wasn't the guy for her.

Sirens sounded in the distance, and an ambulance and fire truck raced by a minute later. The rain was coming down even harder, and Alison was glad she was with Evan. She felt safe with him. As the oldest in her family, she was used to being the one in charge, the one her younger siblings turned to for help and advice. And as a pediatric nurse, she often literally held her patients' lives in her hands. The children she cared for needed her, and their parents relied on her to guide them with some of the most difficult decisions of their lives. It wasn't often that she needed to rely on someone else—or that she'd trust them enough to allow herself to.

Yet despite the crazy storm raging around them, she didn't feel the slightest bit worried with Evan beside her. And what a strange feeling that was. Granted, he probably had more training and responsibilities than most guys his age. The training to become a SEAL was rigorous, and she knew from Rebecca's stories that the guys engaged in strenuous PT and exercises daily. He was probably used to dealing with scenarios she couldn't even imagine. Although she did deal with death in a way most civilians never had to, it certainly wasn't to the extent that guys like Evan did when they deployed. Although she realized she could never know the details about the missions he went on, she wasn't a fool. Those guys risked their lives every time they were sent out.

They came to an accident on the road, both lanes blocked off by police cars with flashing lights. An officer directed them to a side street, and she felt sorry for the man standing outside in the deluge. The bright yellow hooded poncho he wore was likely doing little to keep out the rain.

Evan carefully navigated around the scene, turning down a side road and going around the block. A steady stream of cars was being re-routed because of the accident, and they inched along in Evan's SUV, seeing only the red tail lights of the car ahead of them and sheets of water cascading down the windshield.

"Man, this is a nightmare," Evan muttered.

As they reemerged onto the main road, he glanced over at her, looking concerned. "What kind of car do you drive?"

"An Accord."

"Maybe I should drive you home. I can give you a lift tomorrow if you need a ride to get your car, but this storm is God awful."

"Oh, I can't ask you to do that."

"I'd feel better if I saw you safely to your house," he said, his voice low. "And I don't mind swinging by tomorrow to take you to get your car—promise."

"I guess that might be for the best," she said as thunder boomed above them. "This storm kind of blew in out of nowhere."

"Good. Because I was going to insist on following you home anyway if you still wanted to pick up your car tonight. You shouldn't be out alone in this weather."

"You barely even know me," Alison protested. Despite her resistance, she felt an unexpected surge of warmth at Evan's protectiveness. This guy hardly knew her—sure, his SEAL buddy was dating her best friend, but it's not like he was obligated to see her safely anywhere. And she'd already flat-out told him at the barbeque that she was too old for him. She didn't get the feeling that he was trying to hit on her or change her mind—he was just genuinely concerned.

"There's no way I'm comfortable with letting a woman drive through this storm alone. Especially this late at night."

Alison smiled. "You sound a lot like Patrick."

"He's a good guy, so I'll take that as a compliment."

"It was."

Evan glanced her way, and their eyes briefly met in the darkness. A beat passed before Evan cleared his throat and returned his focus to the road.

"If you're going to go to all that trouble, let me at least cook you dinner tomorrow to thank you."

"Dinner?"

"Sure, why not? As friends," she added, lest he get the wrong idea.

His lips quirked up, and she hoped she hadn't

added that last part unnecessarily. He'd seemed interested in her earlier at the barbeque, and she didn't want to lead him on. Although he was the type of guy that would have offered any stranded woman a ride home, she sensed he was interested in pursuing more with her. While she knew he didn't give her a ride home tonight expecting anything, she didn't want him to get the wrong idea with her dinner invitation and hope for something that was never going to happen between them.

Although she wanted to thank him for his kindness and enjoyed being around him, dating Evan would be another story. A SEAL with dark hair and piercing blue eyes had already caught her attention earlier at the barbeque. She wondered where Brent had disappeared to after they'd chatted and hoped she'd run into him again soon. She'd have to ask Rebecca about Brent tomorrow, maybe even get his number from Patrick. She didn't feel that he'd be too put off by her tracking him down.

"I suppose I could work with that," he teased. Evan was cute with his blond hair and amused grin, not to mention his muscular physique, but he wasn't her type. At all. "Fair warning—you've seen how much I eat."

"Consider me warned. Don't forget—I grew up with two younger brothers. I'll make sure you're well-fed."

A low rumble in the back of his throat had her glancing his way.

She gave him directions to her house and pulled her phone from her purse when she heard it beeping. Typing a quick reply to Rebecca to let her know she was almost home, she put it back into her bag. There was no sense in telling her Evan was giving her a lift. After all, there really wasn't much to tell, was there?

They pulled into her driveway fifteen minutes later. The rain was still coming down, but not nearly as hard as earlier. It looked like the worst had blown over.

"I'll come around and help you out," Evan said, shutting off the engine.

"Don't be silly—you'll get soaked, too."

Evan leveled her with a gaze. "Sit tight."

Alison was too startled at his commanding tone to say anything as he jumped out of the SUV and jogged around to her side. He helped her out of the vehicle and tried to shield her from some of the downpour as they hurried to her front door. There was a rush of water running across the front walk, and before Alison could stop him, Evan swept her into his arms. She gasped in surprise, and a second later, he was setting her down in front of her door. Thankfully the porch was covered, and she felt like they were isolated in their own little world as the skies shattered around them.

"How's that for service?" Evan asked with a grin.

She couldn't help but laugh. He looked so proud that he'd—quite literally—swept her off her feet.

She'd liked the feel of Evan's muscular arms holding her close to his broad chest a little bit too much. The feel of his muscles, the warmth of his skin as he'd held her—for just a split second she'd imagined what it would be like to feel his body caging her in, kissing her, making love to her. If he'd go that much out of his way for a woman he just met, a woman who'd already told him she wanted just to be friends, she wondered what it would be like to date this man. He'd probably be whisking her off of her feet anytime he felt like it.

They stared at each other for a moment, and she felt her heartbeat speed up.

"You're drenched," she said softly, reaching up and quickly brushing some of the water from his face, feeling the slight stubble of his five o'clock shadow beneath her fingertips. For a second, she imagined what the rasp of his whiskers would feel like against her skin—the roughness against the swells of her breasts as he moved over her body, the scraping of that stubble on her inner thighs....

His eyes flared, and she pulled back, offering him a small smile instead. "Just let me know what time works for tomorrow." She had to snap out of this daze he currently had her in. It must just be the adrenaline from the past hour that had her thinking so unclearly. Evan wasn't the guy for her. He never could be.

They made plans for the next day, and before she could stop him, Evan bent down and softly brushed his lips against her forehead. The sparks that shot through her at his tender touch nearly undid her. But the moment was over as soon as it had begun, and Evan turned and ran down the driveway to his SUV. She stood there watching him for a moment, her entire body sizzling at his brief kiss. If she felt this way from a chaste kiss like that, what would it feel like to have his lips on hers? To feel that mouth kissing every inch of her bare skin?

She shuddered, then turned and opened the door before he caught her staring after him. As amazing as the moment was, she couldn't let herself get carried away. She wasn't going to fall for a younger man again. Sure they could have fun together and probably enjoy many passionate nights, but when she wanted to take their relationship to the next level? To settle down or hope to start a family? He'd cut and bail like her ex, and then she'd just be left with nothing but a broken heart all over again.

Chapter 4

Evan jogged along the beach just after sunrise the following morning, adrenaline coursing through his system. He'd spent a restless night tossing and turning in his bed, a certain redhead on his mind. He'd left Alison's house hot and bothered last night—brushing his lips against her forehead had been a mistake, because after that, he'd been unable to shake the memory of her scent. The fruity fragrance she wore clung to her skin, had been surrounding him in his SUV as he drove her home, and had been even stronger when she'd stood right in front of him. He'd wanted to bend lower and devour her, tasting her sweet lips and claiming her mouth with his tongue.

Hell. How was he supposed to play it cool at dinner when the woman was driving him out of his mind? He'd loved tucking her small frame against his chest when he'd carried her to the front door. It wasn't often that he literally swept a woman off her feet, but he hadn't been able to stop himself. With that long skirt she had on, he knew she'd be soaked stepping in that mess. He was being chivalrous, yes, but hell if he didn't love the idea of holding her close to him. And it had felt every damn bit as good as he'd imagined.

Her damp tank top had clung to her curves, the swells of her breasts taunting him. She was small and petite but with womanly curves in exactly *all* the right places. And oh how he longed to explore them further one day. The woman had no idea how completely tempting she'd looked as they'd stood there on her porch. If he wasn't such a gentleman, he'd have invited himself in for a drink. And breakfast the following morning.

He smirked, thinking that was just the style of some of the other guys on his team. Brent, especially. He was aggressive when he went after a woman, and they seemed to all love it. It had been quite the opposite of that last night, with Brent chasing after some other blonde woman. Nah. Brent wasn't interested in his girl. Not that Alison was *his*. But hell, if things went his way, he'd sure like a damn shot.

The phone he'd clipped to his armband vibrated, and he frowned. There weren't many reasons for anyone to be contacting him this early.

Pulling the phone free, he saw it was just Matthew texting him to see if he wanted to meet up at Anchors tonight. Why the hell the message couldn't wait until after breakfast, he had no idea. Maybe Matthew had a sleepless night as well. Evan didn't recall seeing him with any particular lady at the barbeque, but that didn't mean much. Evan had been so caught up in watching Alison all evening, who knew how the other guys had fared.

Alison had put a damper on any thoughts he had of asking her out by inviting him over for dinner as friends. But he was a patient man. A little wooing, and she'd be his in no time. Compared to the way the women usually fell all over him and his buddies at Anchors, the thrill of the chase could be fun. And he had the distinct impression that Alison was a woman who'd love to be caught.

The storm last night had left debris littered all along the shoreline—seaweed, broken shells, and random detritus were scattered across the sand. He moved to the damp, compact sand closest to the water, avoiding the trail of debris left higher up. Anyone coming to the beach would be in for a surprise later on. They'd have to clear an area just to lay their towel down. Then again, high tide would be coming in a few hours, and much of it would be taken back out to sea.

Last night had been surreal. The Virginia Beach area flooded during hurricanes, but that had been just a summer storm blowing in from the ocean. The roads had been covered in several inches of water as he'd driven back home after dropping Alison off. He was glad he'd decided just to take her home—after navigating the streets in his SUV, he wouldn't have felt comfortable letting a woman drive off alone in that deluge. Especially after finding out she only drove a small sedan. It was far too easy to lose control of your vehicle in that type of situation and get swept clear off the road. Plus, he now had the added benefit of seeing her again today.

The dinner invitation had come as a complete surprise. He'd have taken her over to get her car anyway—hell, that's what he'd offered to do in the first place when he'd picked her up outside Patrick's neighborhood. She'd seemed pretty intent on reminding him they were just friends, but that didn't stop his need to pursue her. He'd go with the friendly vibe for a while, maybe sneak in a little harmless flirting. But one of these days, he fully intended on asking her out.

The chemistry between them on her front porch last night only solidified his interest in her. She'd looked so sweet and innocent gazing up at him, her cheeks flushed from running through the rain, her damp tank top clinging to her skin. He'd been a perfect gentleman, bending down for just a friendly kiss across her forehead. It had taken just about everything in him to turn away at that point. She smelled sweet—like oranges, or some other delicious fruit. Those green eyes had gazed up at him, and it was all he could do not to haul her inside her house, making love to her until the morning.

He would've gladly given up his morning run for a night—hell, many nights—in her bed, but he knew she wasn't ready for that yet. Scooping her up into his arms and carrying her through the water had made him hard as a rock. He loved holding her to his chest, protecting her. If cradling her in his arms had felt that good, what would holding her against him so that all of their body parts perfectly aligned feel like? Feeling those breasts pressed up against his chest, her tight heat rubbing against his erection? He'd probably go insane.

Evan didn't even know what Alison did for a living, but he sensed that she liked taking care of people. She'd mentioned a couple of times that she had two younger brothers, so she'd probably grown up watching out for them. Last night she hadn't wanted Evan to walk her to the door because she was worried about *him* getting soaked. Then she'd offered to cook dinner for him since he'd driven her home and was giving her a ride to pick up her car today.

Hell, even if they were just going to be friends, she'd have to get used to Evan doing things for her. It was in his nature to look out for others, to take care of people. And as for an attractive woman like Alison? There was no way he was going to stand around and watch her struggle when he could just as easily offer his assistance.

He glanced down at his watch and groaned. He'd told Alison he'd swing by her place after lunch so they could retrieve her car, but that was hours from now. He ran faster in the sand, his lungs burning as he pushed himself harder. The adrenaline coursing through him at the thought of seeing her again had to be dealt with in one way or another. He didn't think she'd take too kindly to him ravishing her the moment he stepped foot inside her house, so he'd have to pound out his frustration the old fashioned way.

He only hoped he could change her mind about him sooner rather than later.

***

Alison opened the door that afternoon, her heart jolting at the sight of Evan standing there in cargo shorts and a dark tee shirt, a lazy grin on his face. Bronzed skin was set off by his cropped blond hair, but it was those turquoise blue eyes that drew her in.

They were so bright it was practically impossible not to notice them as he watched her. He was holding a small bouquet of flowers, which was both charming and completely unnecessary. Not to mention kind of sweet. She felt a rush of pleasure at his thoughtfulness. He was here helping *her,* taking her to retrieve her car, and he'd brought flowers like they were going out on a date or something.

She smiled and thanked him, taking the colorful arrangement. His fingers brushed against hers, and for just a moment, she remembered him brushing his lips across her forehead the night before. This was *so* not the direction she envisioned the day going, but there you go. Evan had once again managed to surprise her.

She lifted the bouquet and inhaled the intoxicating scent. Mixed in with whatever cologne Evan had on, she was a goner. Would it be too late to suggest she'd just take a cab to pick up her car? That seemed to be a safer bet. Sitting in close quarters in Evan's SUV seemed like the last thing she needed at the moment.

He's too young for you.

Maybe if she told herself that enough times, she could convince her body to sync up with her brain. Something about him had her short-circuiting, imagining they were *together* together and getting ready to do the horizontal tango, not friends who had barely just met.

"Evan, that's so sweet, but you didn't need to bring me flowers."

He shrugged, his broad shoulders rising. His large frame took up her entire doorway, and the shirt he had on hugged his massive chest and well-defined biceps. She tried not to stare, but how exactly had she not noticed how insane his body was last night?

The man was certainly built, and the way he carried himself made her feel like he'd be confident anywhere. Competent, too, she thought as his eyes slid over her. Evan was a man who would know what he was doing in the bedroom. Why that thought suddenly came to mind, she didn't want to focus too closely on. She wasn't going to date Evan or go to bed with him.

A small part of her mind started to riot, chanting *friends with benefits, friends with benefits*. Yeah, like that would lead anywhere close to happily ever after.

She knew the deal with guys like him. All the SEALs on Evan's team attracted women everywhere they went. She'd flirted a bit last night with Brent at the barbeque, long before Evan crossed her radar, but even then she'd known it was a lost cause. She'd heard stories from Patrick that made her feel like she should steer clear of any of them if she knew what was best for her. And she was certain those were the toned-down, PG-13 rated versions.

Unless she was looking to get her heart broken again, a guy like either Brent or Evan was all wrong. If she wanted one night of fun or to become another notch on some guy's bedpost, they'd certainly be up for it. Those guys were nothing but flirts and teases. They chased after women and loved every second of it. Taking a woman home sure didn't mean she was anything special. Or that she'd ever see them again.

Things had worked out for Patrick and Rebecca, but that was more of a rare occurrence than the norm. He was the only man on the team in a serious relationship. The only one who'd ever been married and had any idea what it was like to have a family.

But as for Evan? A young guy like him wouldn't

want a family for years. It could be a decade or more before he was ready to settle down. With the amount of time these guys deployed, Evan wouldn't even be around much. No wonder they were content to find a willing lady at Anchors and then send her on her merry way the next morning. A few orgasms and wham, bam, thank you ma'am. That *sooo* was not her style.

She glanced down at the flowers again. She couldn't even recall the last time a man had brought her flowers. She supposed it would have to have been her ex, and only then on Valentine's Day or something. These were unexpected and...nice.

Evan eyed her as they stood in the doorway, with something like smug satisfaction crossing his face. Those full male lips looked about ready to break into a grin again, and there was a spark in his eyes. Yes, he was definitely pleased that she liked the flowers. "What can I say? I know how to treat a lady who offers to cook dinner for me."

"Yeah—one who offered that because you chauffeured me around all night. This was supposed to be about *me* thanking *you*."

"I'm old-fashioned like that. An attractive woman offers to cook me dinner—I'm bringing flowers."

He winked, and Alison felt heat rising in her cheeks. *No, no, no.* This was not the way things were supposed to be going at all. She was supposed to be acting all big-sister like to him. Friendly. Offering him a warm meal to thank him for his help, and then sending him on his way.

Evan was not supposed to be flirting with her, looking so deliciously tempting, before he'd even stepped foot inside her house. He leaned closer, and she caught a whiff of the aftershave he had on. She was pretty certain he had *not* been wearing that last night. It was spicy and masculine, enticing, and she tried hard not to flinch as the scent of him surrounded her. Or to lean closer and inhale the scent of his neck. Which would be entirely inappropriate given the circumstances.

He brought his large hand to her cheek, his fingers caressing her flushed skin. Heat licked through her, and she was certain she'd turned an even deeper shade of red at her reaction to him. The pads of his fingers were rough, slightly calloused, yet he touched her so gently, she longed to feel them skimming over the rest of her body.

"Shall we go pick up your car?" Evan asked, his blue eyes searching hers.

He looked like he'd do anything she wanted at the moment—jump at her command, take her to dinner, jet them off to Paris... take her to bed. There was a slight longing in Evan's gaze, like he knew he wanted more than she could give.

Too bad he didn't realize *she* was the one who needed more. She'd have to keep him at arm's length simply because she couldn't let anyone like him get too close.

"Yeah," she said, breaking their connection. "Let me just go put these in water first."

She turned, trying to shake off the effect he was having on her. Wow. Had she really been so caught up in Brent last night that she hadn't noticed how insanely attractive Evan was? He'd driven her home for heaven's sake. Maybe she'd been so flustered about nearly getting stranded out in the rain that she hadn't noticed exactly how hot her knight in shining armor had been. Or her SEAL in a souped-up SUV. Still. That didn't mean something was going to happen. They'd get her car, she'd fix him dinner, and that would be that. It wasn't like she'd see him again anytime soon.

Evan followed her into the kitchen, admiring her townhome as they walked along. Alison made a decent salary as a nurse and had been happy to invest in a home of her own. After years spent living with roommates when she was younger, it was nice to have the place to herself. Not that she wouldn't mind a man here—eventually. She just wasn't sure the right guy was even out there.

"Sweet—you have a grill!" Evan exclaimed, grinning like a kid in a candy store as he gazed out on her deck. "Is that a Weber? Someday one of those beauties will be mine."

"You don't have one at your place?" Alison asked, glancing over her shoulder as she filled a vase with water.

"Nope—I'm in an apartment near base with pretty strict rules."

"No grills allowed?"

"Just George Foreman's—totally not the same."

"I guess we could grill tonight…. I was planning to make a vegan tofu stir-fry for dinner though."

Evan literally looked wounded as she snuck a glance his way. Like someone had kicked his puppy dog or something. She bit her lip as she tried not to laugh. She could tell he was trying to be polite and think of a suitable way to respond. He was definitely not the kind of man that would say anything to offend a woman. And he quite likely never *ever* ate tofu.

When he finally met her gaze, she raised her eyebrows. "Or we can have the steaks I picked up earlier."

His blues eyes flared with amusement. Or was that arousal. "You're killing me, Ali."

He sauntered over to where she stood by the sink, looking like a predator stalking his prey. One who would very much enjoy playing with what he caught. Her breathing hitched as she looked up to meet his eyes. He was tall. Broad. Muscular. And grinning wickedly. Before she could think or move out of the way, he reached down, and two large hands wrapped around her waist as he hoisted her up and over his shoulder.

"Evan! Put me down!" she shrieked as her stomach collided with his very broad shoulder and her torso and head dangled down over his back.

"Vegan tofu stir fry," he muttered. "You've got to be kidding me, baby."

Evan was massive—nothing but walls of solid muscle covered by smooth, bronzed flesh. His hands gripped her securely, and their heat burned right through her clothing, sending electricity shooting from her head to her toes. She felt small and feminine, delicate even—the exact opposite of the force that was Evan. He chuckled, knowing exactly what he was doing as she weakly protested and squirmed, struggling to get down. The chances of that were about as likely as her ability to scale Mt. Everest. The man was a mountain, and she was stuck on top.

At least this position did give her a very nice view of his butt. She hadn't planned on inspecting it up close, yet...damn. Was any part of this man not perfection?

He ignored her protests, turning around and loping across the kitchen as his arm snared around her waist, locking her to him. Evan was as solid as a rock. Even though she should be freaking out, dangling over his shoulder like this, somehow she still felt safe. Like Evan was in control and wouldn't let anything harm her.

He acted like she weighed nothing at all, smoothly moving around as if he carried women over his shoulder every day. Maybe he did. Guys like Evan had women crawling all over them. Hadn't Rebecca, who'd sworn she'd never date again, practically swooned over Patrick? That sooo was not happening to her. Ever.

"Keys?" he asked, a smile in his voice.

Damn him for enjoying this so very much.

"Evan, seriously, put me down," she protested as he swung around again, heading toward the table. Was he planning to carry her out to his car like this so all the neighbors could see? How would she explain that?

"Is that your purse?" He snagged it from where it hung on the back of a chair as she laughed harder, watching his muscular grip of her cute little Kate Spade. Really. It wasn't every day that a macho guy like Evan walked around carrying a woman's designer handbag. Then again, he had her slung over his shoulder, caveman style. Maybe that counteracted the purse carrying bit?

"Hmmm…a little girlier than what I usually carry," Evan teased.

"Not your style?"

"Maybe if it were cotton candy pink."

Alison laughed again, unable to get the image of

Evan and a little pink purse out of her mind. Evan tightened his grip as he turned to leave the kitchen, and her fits of laughter soon turned into gasps. She felt dizzy and breathless from the way that he held her, high over his shoulder with her head dangling down. Even though he'd been gentle, she struggled to catch her breath. All the laughing she was doing was not exactly helping, either. But it wasn't every day that a man flung her over his shoulder. She practically expected him to shout out, "Me Tarzan! You Jane!" before hauling her off to bed.

Her asthma had been under control for the past few years, but after fighting off a bout of bronchitis in the spring, she'd needed her inhaler more than usual. Laughing hysterically was only exacerbating the underlying problem. She wheezed and then pounded her fist on Evan's back. He stiffened and instantly lifted her down, a look of alarm crossing his face.

"Are you okay?"

His hands rested on her hips, and if she hadn't been in the middle of an asthma attack, struggling to breathe, she might have enjoyed the feel of his broad body looming in front of her, his large hands spanning her hips, and the concerned way he watched her. He ducked his head lower, trying to meet her gaze.

She reached for her purse, which had fallen to the ground in the commotion, and took another wheezing breath.

"Do you have an inhaler?"

She nodded as tears filled her eyes. Evan tore her purse open, dumping the contents on the kitchen table, and grabbed her inhaler. She snatched it from him with trembling hands. Sinking down onto the chair, she wrapped her lips around the contraption, holding her breath as the icky-tasting medicine filled her mouth. *One…two…three….*

"Shit, Ali, I'm sorry," Evan said, crouching down to look her in the eye. His blue gaze was filled with concern, and his jaw ticked as he ground his teeth. She felt the heat radiating off his large body as he leaned closer, and he rested one hand on her thigh, stroking her reassuringly.

"I didn't realize you had asthma, or I never would've—"

She nodded and dispensed a second pump of the inhaler, feeling relief wash over her as the wheezing began to subside. She just needed to keep her breathing under control, and she'd be a-okay. She wasn't sure if Evan's gentle touch was helping or hindering her. Maybe a little bit of both. Knowing Evan was there right at her side made her feel safe and protected, but the weight of his hand on her thigh also sped up her heart rate.

Conflicting emotions danced through her.

She didn't respond to Evan, and he seemed to understand that she needed a minute. SEALs had medical training, so he must have some clue as to what was happening. He was calm and collected, attuned to her breathing, but he looked angry with himself.

A single tear escaped and rolled down her cheek, brought on more from stress than discomfort or sadness. God, how embarrassing. First she'd had an asthma attack in front of an insanely hot Navy SEAL, and now she was sitting here crying? What next? Maybe she'd trip and fall down the stairs later on, landing on her butt right in front of him. Or somehow catch the kitchen on fire when she was cooking dinner. That might top this in terms of awkward moments.

Even if they were only friends, Evan was the first man she'd had over to her place in months. The only man she'd offered to cook for since her ex shattered her heart. And here she was crying at her kitchen table, barely able to catch a breath.

"God, Alison, I'm a complete jackass. I just threw you over my shoulder like some goddamn caveman—"

"I'm fine." She brushed her tears aside and made a move to stand up.

Evan collected her in his arms and gently pulled her to him. A second later she was seated in Evan's lap, her head tucked against his chest as he held her. Not having the strength or desire to pull away, she relaxed into his solid warmth. His hand rubbed her back, moving in smooth, soothing circles, and she closed her eyes. Evan's heartbeat pounded beneath her ear. His clean, spicy scent surrounded her. He was solid and warm and real.

She could get used to this, this feeling of a man holding her safe and close. Which was dangerous. Evan was sweeter than she'd given him credit for— he'd been interested in her last night and had flirted shamelessly with her earlier today, but this softer side? Caring attention like this would nearly make her come undone.

He knew how to take care of a woman. He probably knew how to drive a woman wild with pleasure, too, but he knew how to be tender. Gentle, even. She hadn't expected that. She knew all the guys on his team had that alpha male instinct to protect others, to fight for those who couldn't defend themselves, but that was more of an aggressive fierceness. A macho need to fight and avenge.

But this? This closeness and tender care she couldn't handle. Maybe Evan *was* the kind of guy looking for a girlfriend, not just some one-night-stand, but that didn't mean he wanted a wife. And she wasn't about to spend a couple years in a relationship with a younger man only to have him break her heart again. Been there, done that. All that was missing were the battle scars to prove it.

Unfortunately, the wounds inside cut just as deep as any physical scars and reminders, and she couldn't give a guy like Evan her heart. Not when she'd barely patched it back together after her last epic failure of a relationship.

Alison let out a small sigh and pulled away. That had felt a little too good allowing Evan to hold her in his arms as if she were something that he could cherish, and it was time to get back to reality. Pick up her car, make him dinner, and then send him on his way. She'd find someone boring, steady, and ready to settle down. Maybe they wouldn't make her heart catapult the way Evan currently was, but they'd never be able to hurt her either.

She started to stand, her hands seeking balance on his broad shoulders. She wasn't sure if it was her asthma attack or his closeness that had her feeling unsteady. All she knew was that her world suddenly was off-kilter.

Evan's hands instantly found her hips again, helping her to rise. He was gentle. Careful. He didn't release her from his grip until she was steady on her own two feet. And it felt better than it should to have his hands on her.

He hopped to his feet in a flash, moving much quicker than she'd think a guy his size could. Must be all that SEAL training. Those guys moved with lightning speed. The contrast between his gentleness and the very-real likelihood that he was positively lethal was confusing. Intriguing. He was a man that would fight to the death if he had to, but he was nothing but careful and considerate around her. There really was more to Evan than met the eye. Too bad she'd never be able to find out the half of it. He'd make some other girl very happy though.

Evan took her hand as she gathered her things, now haphazardly scattered across the table. His grip was solid and secure. His large hand wrapped so carefully around her own, she realized he was more concerned about her than he was letting on. The guy wouldn't even let her step away from his side as she got ready to leave. When she'd finally stuffed her belongings back into her purse, he squeezed her hand gently and tugged her toward the door.

She felt safe. Shielded. Dizzy—and not from the asthma attack earlier. She was confused as all get out as to what was going on with the man standing beside her. The man holding her hand so gently in his own.

Briefly, she met his gaze.

Why did his touch have to feel so good?

Chapter 5

"Are you sure you're okay to pick up your car?" Evan asked for the third time, clicking the remote to unlock the doors to his SUV. He pulled open the door for Alison, watching her carefully. She'd insisted she was fine, but hell if he didn't feel like the biggest jerk on earth for causing her asthma attack. Or at least contributing to it. She'd insisted her illness earlier in the year had left her vulnerable to more frequent bronchial spasms. Or some shit like that. It turned out that Alison was a nurse at the hospital, so she sure as hell knew more than him when it came to medicine. Not that that made him feel better at the moment.

Seriously. What the hell was wrong with him?

She'd asked him not once, but *twice* to put her down, but he was too busy enjoying playing the role of big, bad SEAL, tossing her over his shoulder. The way she'd laughed hysterically let him know she'd liked it, too. He's seen Alison checking him out when she thought he wasn't looking. And when he'd hauled her up against him?

She was soft and feminine compared to his tall, muscular frame and hell if he didn't love the contrast. The feel of her warm body up against his had made him want to haul her off to her bedroom. Forget the damn car. He'd take care of *all* her needs, pleasuring her until she was sated. Then he'd order delivery so they could eat dinner together before round two. And three.

But had he listened when she'd said to put her down? Not a chance. He'd grabbed her purse, prepared to head for the front door. With Alison still slung over him. It was only when he realized she was gasping for air that he released her. And felt like the biggest dick in the world.

"Evan, I promise, I'm fine. I have asthma. Sometimes I have asthma attacks, which is why I carry an inhaler. It's not a big deal."

"Maybe I should call one of the guys to meet us down there. They can drive your car back, and you can ride with me."

"Evan."

He sighed. There was no arguing with Alison now that her mind was made up. She'd just spent the past ten minutes assuring him she was okay. He just hoped she wasn't putting on a brave face for him, trying to look stronger than she was. Then again, her breathing had returned to normal. She wasn't gasping or coughing or whatever that was. What the hell did he know about inhalers or asthma? Alison was the one with a nursing degree. Although he'd been trained in field medicine, his knowledge was more about patching up bullet wounds on the battlefield and applying tourniquets to bleeding soldiers. But treating respiratory problems? Not exactly.

"Fine. But I'm cooking dinner."

"Evan!"

He climbed into the driver's side of the SUV and flashed her a grin. "No protests. I'm cooking, or we're not eating."

Alison rolled her eyes.

"Are you always so feisty?" he asked as he backed down the driveway. She was cute when she was mad. Did she think that little pout was going to change his mind or something? No chance in hell.

"Are you always so bossy?"

Evan sighed. "Do we need to swing by the grocery store after we get your car?"

"No, I walked over this morning and bought a few things."

Evan nearly slammed on the brakes. "You walked?"

"It's just down the block."

"But you have asthma."

Alison laughed. "Seriously Evan, I'm not an invalid. Guess what? I exercise, too. And do yard work. And take care of patients at the hospital."

"All right, all right. I'm sorry. But we could've gone together."

"I was trying to do something nice for you, remember?"

He relaxed a little. She could walk down the street. There was no need to go all alpha male on her. "You just really freaked me out earlier."

"Look, I appreciate your worry. But I know my limits. I just couldn't catch my breath before, and all the laughing wasn't exactly helping."

"Yeah, what was so damn funny anyway?" Not that he hadn't enjoyed her laughter. It had spurred him on even more. Making her smile like that had made him feel about ten feet tall. But no way was he pulling a stunt like that again at the expense of her safety. Illness or not, if just laughing brought on an asthma attack, he'd have to be careful.

"You looked pretty cute holding my purse."

"Cute, huh?" He raised his eyebrows and glanced over at her, a gleam in his eye. Was that a hint of a blush starting on her cheeks?

"Don't push your luck."

***

An hour later, Evan was flipping steaks on the grill at Alison's townhouse. Alison's Accord was safely parked in her driveway, right next to his SUV, like they both belonged there or something. When he'd pulled in next to her and she'd flashed him a smile, his heart had stopped for a second. It was like some weird déjà vu, alternate universe type thing. Like he'd done it a thousand times before. Things were easy with her, and he'd just met the girl—officially—last night. How crazy was that.

The lady at the impound lot had tried to charge Alison for the tow, but he'd flashed a grin her way and fed her some mumbo-jumbo about serving his country. They'd been in the wrong, not Alison, but sweetening up the woman at the counter certainly hadn't hurt. Yep, the SEAL bit had the ladies eating out of his hand every time. Alison had been oddly silent during the exchange. Huh.

The smell of the steaks on the grill drew his attention back to the present. They sizzled, making his mouth water, and he grinned. He glanced around the courtyard her townhome backed up to. Green grass, lots of trees. Even a swing set for the kids. He'd love a place of his own, but with so many deployments and his still-single status, it seemed a bit pointless. Why buy a house when he had no one to fill it?

His apartment near base was all a guy like him needed. Aside from the wife and two point five kids he hoped to have someday. He smirked. Who came up with that shit anyway? A solid three kids would be cool with him.

Alison was inside the kitchen making some kind of chick salad to go along with dinner, but she'd also made some killer guacamole, so he'd let the salad part slide. Women.

He watched her through the sliding glass doors as she worked. She'd pulled that long, strawberry blonde hair up into a ponytail. It swished around as she walked. Back and forth. Back and forth. Man, that woman was mesmerizing, and she had no clue what she did to him. Alison grabbed two beers from the fridge, and blood rushed to his groin as he watched her bend over in those skinny jeans she had on. Her heart-shaped ass was a sight to see, and he longed to palm it, running his hands over those sweet curves, pulling her close, and never letting her go.

His phone buzzed in his pocket, and he shook off that thought. Glancing at the screen, he saw a text from Christopher.

You coming tonight, Flip?

Hell. He'd texted Matthew back earlier this

morning but kept it vague. Anchors was a no go. He wasn't sure he wanted them knowing he was over at Alison's. Not that he had a problem spreading that news to the world, but she seemed skittish about pursuing anything other than friendship with him. No sense in spooking the woman, especially when they had mutual friends. Or, rather, when her best friend was dating a dude on his SEAL team. Maybe that was his ticket. He'd suggest they hang out with Patrick and Rebecca next weekend. It wouldn't have to be a date, just a few friends getting together.

"Do you want to eat inside or out?" Alison asked, her cheeks looking flushed as she poked her head out the door. She coughed once as the smoke from the grill blew her way, and Evan frowned.

"Inside."

She didn't notice the expression on his face and ducked back in to grab the plates from the cupboard. A cursory glance at the steaks let him know they'd be okay for a few minutes without his attention, and he slipped in the side door.

Actually, sneaking up on her was decidedly *not* a good idea. He didn't want to cause another asthma attack. Not that surprise caused them, did it? He'd have to do some research online tonight. The next time she couldn't breathe around him, he wanted to know exactly how to help her.

"Need a hand?"

Green eyes glanced at him from over her shoulder. "Uh, yeah. Can you grab that platter for the steaks?"

"Sure thing."

She turned back around, and a second later he was right behind her. She still had that insane fruity fragrance that drove him out of his mind. What was that? Her perfume? Some fancy shampoo? No matter. He was hard as a rock—had been earlier as he watched her bend over to get the beers.

He was careful not to let himself rub up against her sweet ass, tempting as though it was. Like that wouldn't freak her out. Still, he let his chest brush up against her back, and he didn't miss the shiver that coursed through her at his sudden closeness. She was warm, sweet, and irresistible. His arms snaked around her, and his hands rested on the counter, trapping her. The cool granite was a complete contrast to his heated flesh, and he froze.

Next move was hers. If she wanted him, she had him.

A beat passed with neither of them moving a muscle. Her breathing quickened, and his own body pulsed with awareness. She was silent, and he would've killed to know what was going on in her head right now. Just a glimpse inside to see if she felt any of the chemistry and connection that he did.

Her silence spoke volumes. She didn't move a muscle, but he could almost hear her heartbeat speed up with every quickened breath she took.

"I could get used to this," he said, his voice gruff as he ducked his head down toward her ear. The slight hitch in her breathing told him all he needed to know.

He affected her. Just as she affected him. She could deny it as much as she wanted, but she was into him, too.

"Evan." The breathless way she said his name was something he'd never tire of hearing. Hell, there were a whole lotta things about this woman that he could see making part of his daily routine. Making her breakfast in the morning. Making dinner together in the kitchen. Making love all night.

"Yes, baby?" His lips teased the shell of her ear, oh-so-close but not quite touching. She actually shuddered.

"We can't."

"We can't what?"

"We're better off just being friends."

He didn't say a word, deciding how to play this. Did he turn her around and prove her wrong? Back off and leave? Go with the "just friends" thing for now?

"We're just standing in your kitchen," he teased, deciding on the latter. The gravel in his voice betrayed him, but he kissed the top of her head as he pulled back, leaving her space. She turned around, and there was no mistaking the flush spreading across her cheeks or the arousal in her eyes.

He grabbed the platter from the top shelf and handed it to her. "I'll go check on the steaks." He winked before turning around and forcing himself to walk away.

Chapter 6

"You should take off Mondays more often," Alison said to Rebecca the next afternoon as she dipped her toes in the pool under the hazy, late afternoon sun. *Ahhh. Perfect.* Cool water. Clear blue skies. Margaritas perched on the table between their lounge chairs. This was the stuff summer was about. All that was missing were some cute cabana boys. Rebecca, of course, only had eyes for Patrick. Too bad those guys were all on base today doing drills. They'd look mighty fine shirtless and in swim trunks, fetching them drinks.

Including Evan, whose image was now seared into her mind. That chiseled physique of his felt rock solid beneath his clothes. She'd probably give in if she ever saw the man partially unclothed. He was way too tempting—in more ways than one. Aside from being hotter than sin, he was sweet to her. Gentle. And, as she decided already, way, way too young.

Alison stepped into the pool, letting the water surround her. Her dark green bikini made her fair skin look even paler—the curse of being a redhead. Despite hours clocked in at the beach and pool this summer, she slathered on the sunblock each time and was pale as a ghost. Unlike Rebecca, who looked like some sort of bronzed brunette goddess lounging on a chair. *Patrick was a lucky man.* Her best friend was a knockout, and Alison couldn't help but feel slightly self-conscious in comparison. She was petite and slender and wouldn't mind Rebecca's killer curves. Not that Evan had seemed bothered in the slightest by her small frame. If anything, he seemed to enjoy picking her up and hauling her around.

Her mind skipped back to him caging her in at her kitchen counter last night, those muscular arms trapping her as his broad chest brushed up against her back. She could feel his solid pecs, tight abs, and scorching heat. She'd actually shivered at his closeness. He was all man and ready to do whatever she'd wanted. All she'd needed to do was say the word, and the night would have ended much differently. The look of lust filling his blue gaze as she'd turned around was almost enough to make her change her mind about him. To throw caution to the wind and allow him to kiss her senseless and drive her out of her mind.

Almost.

If only she was young enough for a summertime fling—Evan would top that list by a long shot. And who was she kidding? She'd been going through a dating drought recently. The accountant she'd gone out with a few times wouldn't even be *on* the list.

She sighed, splashing a little water up onto her

arms and shoulders to cool off. The heat of the sun felt good on her skin. Warm. Comforting. Drops of water cascaded down her arms, and she remembered shivering in Evan's car the other night as she escaped the rain. Without even saying a word, he'd turned down the air conditioning, noticing she was cold. Without her even asking him for help, he'd been the one to pull to a stop and offer her a ride.

He was a great guy that someone would be lucky to end up with. It just couldn't ever be her.

"Long weekends are made for summertime," Rebecca agreed, sipping her margarita. "Wow, that's strong. How much tequila did you put in these?"

"Enough."

"Guess I'll be sticking to one."

"That's okay—more for me," Alison joked.

"No fair, you don't have to drive home—or work tomorrow."

"There are definite perks to my shift," Alison agreed. "But I don't feel too bad about you returning home to a smoking hot man."

Rebecca blushed and glanced over to make sure her daughter wasn't listening. Abby was a few feet away, happily arranging her pool toys on an empty lounge chair and didn't so much as look up.

Alison climbed out of the water, a smile playing on her lips, and sank down onto the lounge chair beside her best friend. She didn't begrudge Rebecca for being happy. But she wouldn't mind if a little of that bliss headed her way. Maybe Evan had an older brother or something? Nah, that would feel weird after the surprising attraction she was feeling toward Evan. There were other guys on his SEAL team though. She'd have to ask Rebecca if anyone was worth learning more about.

The sooner she found someone else, the sooner she'd get Evan out of her mind.

"I wouldn't know what a few days off felt like if it smacked me in the face," Rebecca said, settling back into her chair. Her embarrassment had faded, but she still looked happily blissed out. Maybe that's what amazing orgasms every night did for you, Alison thought with a smirk. Rebecca wasn't one to kiss and tell, but Alison knew she was smitten with her new man. And satisfied, if the glow she was sporting twenty-four/seven said anything about it.

"So take a vacation."

"Maybe."

"You and Patrick could go somewhere."

"We could—it's tough to coordinate our schedules though."

A busy lawyer at a law firm in Virginia Beach, Rebecca worked insane hours. Alison and Rebecca met for dinner from time-to-time, but a weekday afternoon spent lounging around the pool like this was practically unheard of. Alison's three-days-on, four-days-off work schedule for her job at the hospital let her relax and unwind when she was off the clock. But as for Rebecca? The woman never seemed to slow down. That was the advantage of being a nurse—once your shift ended, so did your work. It wasn't like she could care for patients at home. Rebecca brought stacks of paperwork home each night, whereas Alison came home from grueling twelve-hour shifts and crashed.

Alison thought her best friend deserved a little R&R after a couple of intense court cases last spring. Rebecca was always dealing with high-strung clients—

divorce didn't bring about the best in people. One of the court hearings had culminated with a stalker chasing after Rebecca. The disgruntled ex-husband of a woman Rebecca had represented at a divorce hearing had sought Rebecca out in revenge. Luckily, Patrick had literally swooped in and saved the day, but not without a lot of drama on the relationship front.

Their break-up hadn't lasted long, but it had been hard on Alison to see her friend so heartbroken. Luckily all's well that ends well. The two of them were now the happiest couple she'd ever seen. Patrick was head-over-heels in love with Rebecca, and seeing Patrick melt all over Rebecca had softened Alison up—a little. She still had trouble trusting relationships to work, but theirs certainly seemed to be smoothly sailing along.

"Truth be told," Rebecca continued, "I wouldn't mind another weekend at a hotel right here in Virginia Beach. That night Patrick and I spent in an oceanfront suite? Definitely one of the best in my life."

Alison grinned at her friend. "That good, huh?"

"Let's just say there were multiples of everything."

Alison giggled. Rebecca was usually so conservative, it was a little surprising to hear her even mentioning sex at all. Maybe Patrick had unleashed a wilder side in her, she thought.

"What's so funny?" Rebecca asked.

"Just wondering if all the guys on Patrick's SEAL team are as thorough as him."

"Uh, have you seen the way women chase after them? That's pretty much a guarantee."

A feeling of unease washed over Alison. It was fun joking about the men's sexual prowess, but actually imagining Evan with another woman didn't sit well with her.

"So...next week. Same time, same place?" she asked, hoping her friend didn't mind the change of subject.

"I wish."

Alison shot her a grin. "Hey, it was worth a shot."

Rebecca snatched a chip from the bowl, shading her eyes with a hand as she looked around. "Have you seen my sunglasses?"

"Right here Mommy!" Rebecca's four-year-old daughter screamed. The whole neighborhood probably heard the kid, but hey. At least she looked cute trying on her mom's oversized shades. She'd filled up her toy watering can and was currently sprinkling pool water on all the flowerpots in the landscaped area. Alison wasn't sure how the plants would fare with all that chlorine, but at least she was happy. It gave her and Rebecca a little girl time to chat and catch up.

"So how'd you do getting home Saturday night?" Rebecca asked. "That storm was insane. I almost called to see if you wanted to stay with me over at Patrick's."

"Yeah, because that wouldn't have been awkward with me as the third wheel. Actually, my car got towed."

"What!" Rebecca shot up from her lounge chair, staring at Alison with wide eyes. "Why didn't you call me? How'd you get home?"

"I was about ready to run back to Patrick's house to find you—or to beg Patrick for a ride home. Evan pulled up a second before the skies broke and offered me a lift."

"Wow. Evan, huh? He's sweet."

"Yeah. I thought I was more into the tall, dark, and brooding type, but he surprised me."

"How so?"

"Drove me home. Came back yesterday to pick up my car from the impound lot with me. I made dinner for him last night."

"Wait—you two had dinner together?"

"We're just friends," Alison said with a laugh. "I just wanted to thank him. I mean he's cute, yes—well, really more like smoking hot. But he's too young for me."

"He's not *that* young."

"You're one to talk. Evan is only like twenty-five or so. Patrick must be like ten years older than him!"

Rebecca shrugged. "I'm pretty sure Evan's older than that. And with the stuff those guys deal with? Even if he is young, he's definitely more mature than other guys his age."

Alison snorted. "Right. I've heard the stories you've told me about Patrick's SEAL team. A different woman every weekend, right?"

"They're not all like that."

"Patrick's the exception; I get it. He's a great guy. But as for the rest of them? I don't think I could hope for anything serious with any of them."

"All of them have been nothing but polite to me."

"Yeah—because Patrick would kill them if they so much as looked at you the wrong way."

Rebecca shrugged, obviously unable to disagree. Of course those guys would treat her with nothing but the utmost respect. From the beginning, Patrick had made it clear to everyone that he cared for Rebecca. He wasn't the type of man to play games, and it's not like his team would go after Patrick's woman. Aside from that, once the rest of the guys on his SEAL team had been informed of Rebecca's stalker, they'd been on her twenty-four/seven, protecting Rebecca *and* her daughter.

Alison was glad that Rebecca had someone to watch over her. But one man's behavior did not foretell how the other guys would act. "I think Evan's interested in me, but I just can't do that again, you know?"

"He's not your ex."

"I don't know. I just don't see it happening." Alison took another sip of her drink and glanced around the pool area. Rebecca knew more than anyone how wary Alison was to get in a relationship again. Her ex had proclaimed she was "the one." Alison had suggested moving in together as the next step, and then *bam*. He'd told her he needed to see the world before he settled down—no need for her to stick around and wait for him.

The guy had broken her heart, and in the two years since, she'd dated but never let anyone get that close to her again. When she did find the right guy, she knew he'd be older. Established. Have a house of his own, a career, and be ready to start a family. She didn't have time for games with boys. Cute as though he was, she shouldn't even waste time thinking of Evan anymore.

"Yeah, come to think of it, Patrick mentioned Evan had a date with some hot brunette chick tonight," Rebecca mused.

"What?" Alison asked, nearly toppling over the table between their two lounge chairs. She grabbed her margarita as it tipped precariously on the edge.

"Don't care, huh?" Rebecca winked.

"I hate you."

"That's what best friends are for."

Chapter 7

Alison groaned at the end of her shift on Friday evening. Her back hurt, her feet hurt, and a long hot shower was about all she wanted at the moment. Maybe that plus some Advil. Twelve hours nonstop in a crazy ER was a hell of a way to start her weekend. Her schedule of Wednesday through Friday at the hospital allowed her plenty of days off to recover in between shifts, but at the moment, all she wanted to do was crash in her bed for the next twenty-four hours or so. Maybe by Sunday she'd be ready to face the world again.

She grabbed her purse from her locker, pulling out her cell phone. She noticed a text from Rebecca.

Patrick and I are grilling tonight at my place. Want to join us?

Huh. She'd hung out with Patrick and Rebecca alone all of once before. They'd just started dating, and it wasn't like they needed a third wheel. Why'd they suddenly want her to come over tonight?

She was getting ready to decline the invitation when her phone buzzed again.

Don't say no! I owe you for having Abby and me over on Monday.

Alison sighed. Margaritas, chips, and apple juice for Abby hardly called for her best friend to invite her over for dinner. Although she loved their girl time, if Patrick was going to be there, too, it meant something else was up. She had a feeling it had something to do with a certain six-foot-two blond Navy SEAL. Patrick wasn't the type of man interested in setting people up, so of course it was all Rebecca's doing. She never should have mentioned having Evan over for dinner last weekend. Her best friend was far too observant for her own good.

So what if Alison thought the guy was cute? Or even insanely attractive—for a younger man. That didn't mean she should date him. Would it be totally rude to decline the dinner invite? He had gone out of his way to help her last weekend, and if Evan thought she'd be there at Rebecca's, a tiny part of her didn't want to let him down. What that feeling was about she didn't care to examine too closely. But seriously, after twelve hours in the ER, she wanted nothing more than a hot shower and her bed. Dinner and a pseudo date hadn't exactly been in the game plan for tonight.

Her cell phone rang as she walked out the hospital doors, and without even bothering to see who was calling, she said, "Hun, I'm way too tired to have dinner with you tonight."

"Wow, I hadn't even asked you yet," a deep voice replied. Evan. "And for someone who keeps insisting we're just friends, should you really be calling me 'hun'?"

Her face heated, the sound of his masculine voice resonating down to her bones. Of course Evan was somehow in on this, too. The whole world was conspiring against her. Why couldn't he be a few years older than her instead? He'd have sewn his wild oats, seen the world—all right, as a SEAL, he probably had. She'd give him that. But he'd be marriage material then. The type of man she could give a chance because they had potential for a future.

Evan might make a cute-as-hell boyfriend now, but she had to think long term. And protect her heart. No way was she dating a guy for a few years again only to have him decide he wasn't ready to settle down. That he didn't want *her*.

"Sorry, I thought you were Rebecca," she muttered.

"Not a chance," he said, clearly enjoying himself. "But as you know, she and Patrick are having a few people over."

"Who?"

"Me. Christopher. His date. You."

"Uh huh. That sounds suspiciously like a bunch of couples having dinner together."

Evan laughed. "So can I convince you to come? Or do I have to pick up some other chick and introduce her to the guys instead?"

"Some other chick?"

"I can't be the only single guy there. You'd be doing me a favor."

"Right," she said, a smile playing on the corner of her lips. Thank God he couldn't see her right now. Evan was entirely too persuasive for his own good.

"That, and what if you need a ride home again? With your luck, your car could be towed right from Rebecca's driveway. I don't want some other man driving you home. Tell you what—I'll pick you up, save you the worry."

Alison laughed. "I'm still at the hospital and need to go home and change."

"So…I'll pick you up in an hour?"

"Yes. One hour."

"Any chance you'll wear that skirt you had on last weekend?" Evan asked hopefully.

"From the barbeque?" she asked, puzzled.

"That's the one." She could practically see the grin on his face.

"What was so special about that skirt?"

"I loved watching you move around in it all night," he admitted, his voice low and practically oozing sex appeal.

"Evan!" Her face flamed. Obviously he wasn't going to tone down the flirting. Was she leading him on by agreeing to go to dinner? It was just her best friend's house, so it wasn't like an official date or something. Was it?

"You're gorgeous, Ali," he said, his voice softer than before.

She bit her lip to keep from smiling. "I'll see you in an hour, tough guy."

"Tough guy?" he asked, chuckling.

"One hour." She hung up and glanced at the time. Crap. She had to get moving.

***

Patrick's cool blue gaze shot to Evan and Alison as

they walked into Rebecca's home. He looked over at Rebecca, raising his eyebrows, and she grinned. Hell, they seemed on board with the idea of Evan and Alison as a couple. Now if only Evan could convince her.

He rested his hand on the small of Alison's back, guiding her into the room. No doubt she'd probably been there a million times before, but he liked touching her. Keeping her close.

She hadn't worn the same skirt as last weekend but instead had on a long dress that skimmed her curves. A "maxi dress," she'd called it, whatever the hell that was. She looked hotter than anything though, her strawberry blonde hair trailing down her back. The dark blue of the dress contrasted with her fair skin, and the swish of her hips and her ass as she walked was driving him out of his mind. It was almost like she sashayed around in that thing just to taunt him. Something about the way she was all covered up yet displaying those womanly curves to their full advantage was as hot as hell.

"Come in," Rebecca said. "Christopher's coming over soon, too, with his date. The kids are already asleep, so I thought we could eat out on the patio."

"Sounds perfect," Alison said, handing her friend a bottle of white wine.

They walked outside to Rebecca's backyard, and Evan again wished he had a nice place of his own. His apartment suited his bachelor status just fine, but he would love to have a yard to mow, a grill to throw some steaks or burgers on, and a wife and kids to come home to. He'd never envied the other men on his SEAL team before, but hell if he wouldn't love for his life to mirror Patrick's. The single life had suited

Evan just fine for the first twenty-seven years of his life, but lately, seeing other men with wives and families had made his gut clench just a little bit in envy.

Alison sat down at the patio table as Rebecca poured the women glasses of wine, and Patrick lit the grill. "Beer's in the fridge, buddy," he called over his shoulder. Evan ducked inside to grab a long neck, and when he came back out, saw Christopher had arrived with a date. Not the same chick he'd brought to the barbeque last weekend, he noted.

Alison was rubbing her shoulders with one hand, tilting her head from side to side. He set his beer down on the table beside her and caught her hand. She glanced up at him in confusion, but he released her and rested his hands on her slender shoulders. Light freckles dusted across her fair skin, and he had this crazy urge to lean down and kiss every single one. Not that he'd be doing that in the middle of Rebecca's backyard—or anytime soon with the way things had been going. At a freaking snail's pace. But if slow and steady got him the girl, he could work with that for the time being.

He lightly massaged Alison's shoulders, feeling her momentarily tense up and then relax into him. "Wow, you're in the wrong profession," she sighed.

"How's that?" Evan asked as the others chuckled.

"If the SEAL thing doesn't work out, you could be a masseur."

"I'm sure the women would be lining up around the block for that," Christopher's date said with a laugh. Evan grinned at her but noticed Alison tensed slightly.

He ducked down, murmuring into her ear, "Only

for you, baby." He massaged lower, between her shoulder blades, and a small moan escaped her lips. Thank God the rest of them were listening to Patrick and Christopher tell some story about training earlier in the day. That little sound coming from Alison's mouth was sexy as fuck.

Evan glanced down, admiring the swell of her breasts just peeking out from the neckline of her dress. His position behind her gave him a glorious view. They were pert, tight, and he could see just a hint of black lace. Holy hell. What he wouldn't give to slowly undress her one of these days, discovering her body. With his hands, with his mouth...with his tongue. Would she taste as sweet as she smelled?

He looked over at the others, not wanting to make her uncomfortable. Her eyes had been shut, and she had no idea he'd been gazing down at her. If he was going to be standing around ogling her breasts, she was going to know about it. Preferably, encouraging him to do more than just look.

The scent of meat on the grill sent his stomach rumbling. Christopher had his arms wrapped around the woman he brought, and they were standing by Patrick, who flipped the burgers. Rebecca was carrying some side dishes out on a tray. Damn those two were domestic and cuter than hell together.

He smirked. Patrick would love that shit. No one would dare tell "Ice" he was cute. He sure seemed smitten with Rebecca though.

"Be right back, babe," he said to Alison as he watched Rebecca struggle with the large load. "I'm going to help Rebecca for a sec." He strode over and took the overflowing tray from her.

"Thanks Evan. You're a real sweetheart."

"Thanks for having us over. As soon as I get a real place, I'll have you and Patrick over sometime."

"And Alison?" she teased, her eyes lighting up.

"Put in a good word for me, okay?" he asked with a wink.

"Already on it."

He set the tray down as Rebecca wandered back over to the grill, wrapping her arms around Patrick. She rested her head on his back, and Evan smiled. Hell if he wouldn't love if Alison acted that way around him some day— too in love with him to resist being away from his side for even a minute.

He grabbed a chair next to Ali, where she relaxed, sipping her wine. She had a cute sprinkling of freckles across her nose that he hadn't noticed before. "Rough day?"

"Just more ER craziness," she said, flashing him a sweet smile.

"You like taking care of people," he noted.

"Yeah. That's what nurses do, I suppose. I already told you I have two younger brothers—I guess maybe it's just second nature at this point."

"And who takes care of you?" he asked, his voice gruff.

"I can take care of myself," she said with a shrug. "I don't need anyone to take care of me." Her voice faltered with her second statement, almost as if she didn't quite believe the way it sounded herself.

"Everyone needs someone, Ali. Maybe I need to take care of you."

Her mouth parted slightly as she gazed over at him.

"Let me take you out sometime. On a real date. Not this dinner with friends and SEAL buddies stuff.

I want you alone."

She bit her lip, and the sight of her teeth sinking into that soft flesh nearly made him come undone. He longed to sink his teeth into her lower lip. To nibble on it and kiss her softly, sweetly. If he thought for a second that she'd allow it, he'd haul her into his arms right now. Hold her close. Kiss that soft skin on her neck and shoulders. Gently bite her lip and soothe the sting with his tongue.

She looked away for a moment, watching the other couples near the grill. They laughed at something Christopher said, and Evan felt like he and Alison were in their own little world for the moment.

Her eyes wandered back to his, and they were bright. Interested.

"Maybe."

He grinned.

***

"So what's going on with you and Evan?" Rebecca whispered later in the evening as Patrick and Evan cleaned up. She had her wine glass in one hand, Alison's elbow in the other, and steered her to the corner of the yard. Christopher had already left with his date, and Rebecca had tugged Alison off under the auspices of showing her some flowers.

At ten o'clock at night.

"I don't know," Alison said, taking a sip of wine. This was her third glass over the course of several hours, but it was still giving her a small buzz. "He's cute. Probably all wrong for me." Her stomach had been doing crazy little flips all evening—starting with walking in the door of Rebecca's together like they were a couple or something, continuing when he'd massaged her neck and shoulders, and ending with him helping to clean up, shooting her searing gazes all the while.

"He's really nice…not to mention totally gorgeous."

"Yeah, and totally too young."

"Patrick was a little confused when I said we should invite some of the guys over tonight—specifically Evan."

"Men can be so dense sometimes."

"Evan seems really into you—that massage he gave you earlier? I'm pretty sure I almost melted watching you two."

"Uh huh. When he had his hands all over my skin? It definitely made me want things I'm not supposed to with a guy like him."

"They're good guys," Rebecca insisted.

"I know—it just caught me by surprise."

"It happens," Rebecca said with a shrug. "I totally wasn't expecting for Patrick to walk into my life. Honestly, I didn't even think I'd ever really date again. But when these guys want something they go after it."

"It being you?" Alison asked with a giggle.

"Is that so bad?" Rebecca teased. "Patrick was pretty intense, but after our first night together? I couldn't imagine ever being with another man again."

Alison grinned. "Some of us don't move at the speed of light like you two. I need to figure things out first."

"Well don't take too long, sweetie. Some things are worth risking our hearts for."

Chapter 8

For the second week in a row, Evan drove Alison home. He liked her beside him in the darkened interior of his SUV. It felt right—like she belonged there or something. How crazy was that? For a man used to being alone, with a history of spending only a night or two with a woman, he sure the hell loved having Alison around.

She yawned, and he glanced over at her profile in the moonlight. She'd closed her eyes for a moment and didn't notice the way his swept over her, taking in her delicate features, gorgeous hair, and the swell of her breasts. His eyes trailed down, her legs covered by that long dress she had on. Fucking gorgeous.

He was more than a little curious about what she and Rebecca had been chatting about after dinner. They both kept shooting glances his way, and he'd started to feel like a kid at the seventh grade dance or something—boys on one side of the yard, girls on the other.

Except Alison was a smoking hot woman. Nothing girlish about her.

And his thoughts veered far beyond asking the girl across the floor to dance. He'd wanted to haul her into his arms, kissing her until she was breathless. Slowly peeling that dress off of her until he saw *all* of that sexy, lacy lingerie he'd noticed peeking out from beneath her dress. Until he'd explored every dip and curve of her.

He adjusted in his seat, his groin becoming tight.

She finally looked over at him and smiled. "I had fun tonight. Thanks for convincing me to have dinner at my best friend's house."

Evan laughed. "Yeah, it was good to see Rebecca and Patrick. That was far from the highlight of my night though." His voice was deeper than he'd intended, and he wondered if Alison knew just how much she affected him.

"Is that so?"

"Hell yeah." His eyes heated as he glanced over at her again.

The smile playing on her lips was dangerous. She looked like the cat that had got the canary. Her green eyes flashed as they passed under a streetlamp. "Hmmm…I can't decide what the highlight of my night was."

He reached ever and snatched her hand, bringing it up to his lips. He brushed a soft kiss across the back of it, and Alison's mouth dropped open in surprise. Holding it there a beat too long, he kissed it again. It was far from chaste and innocent the way his lips continued to brush against her skin, and the fact that Alison didn't pull away told him plenty.

***

Alison climbed out of Evan's SUV ten minutes later, listening to him grumbling beside her that he'd get the door. Ha. Like she couldn't climb out of his damn car unassisted.

That kiss had been scorching—and all the man had done was brush his lips across her hand. She was in way, way too deep already. The crazy thing was, hardly a damn thing had happened. They'd had dinner a few times. Flirted a bit. But it wasn't exactly like Rebecca and Patrick's first date where they'd spent the night making love in a luxury hotel suite.

Not that Rebecca had volunteered all the details, but with the satisfied smile on her lips all the time? The woman was happier than she'd been in ages.

"Couldn't wait for me to help you, huh?" Evan smirked, crossing his arms in mock irritation. She loved the way his muscles bulged when he stood like that. Thick biceps, corded forearms, muscular hands that she wouldn't mind him dragging all over her skin.

Damn he was cute acting all chauvinistic and macho on her.

She shrugged, flashing him a knowing smile.

Evan driving her home was quickly becoming a routine she wouldn't mind getting used to. He was attentive and sweet. Hotter than any man she'd ever dated. He asked her questions about her work at the hospital. About her family.

And when those bright blue eyes bore into hers?

She loved it even more than she cared to admit.

He was so, so wrong for her, yet her body was screaming he was so, so right.

She turned to walk toward the front door as he assessed her, and a second later he'd captured her in his arms. She squealed in delight as he swung her up against his broad chest—not over his shoulder like last weekend, she noted. Evan holding her right against his solid, muscular frame was even better though. She felt protected and safe. Feminine, as he held her like she weighed nothing at all.

Part of her wanted to tug that shirt right off him, exploring the ripples of muscles on his abdomen, the broad pectorals spanning his chest, and the bulging biceps that held her. She wanted to trail over every hard plane and dip with her fingertips. To brush over them with her lips.

Ripples of desire shot through her as he held her close. He was in charge, commanding the situation, handling her. And hell if she didn't love it.

No way was she sleeping with him tonight though. She'd had a few drinks, a long couple of days, and a lot of soul-searching to do.

Evan set her down right in front of her door and lifted her chin so that she met his searching gaze. "Part of me wants to invite myself in," he admitted. "But I don't think you're ready for that."

"No," she said, smiling as he caressed her cheek with his fingers.

"Do you look at all of your male 'friends' the way you're staring up at me now?" he asked, his voice gruff.

"No," she admitted, warmth spreading through her.

"Good."

He stepped back, waiting for her to unlock her door. She glanced over her shoulder at him. Heat licked through his eyes, his body tense. Their eyes locked, and she was pretty sure her heart stopped beating for a moment. Fumbling with the key, she finally unlocked the door and pushed it open. She didn't hear him move, but as she turned to say goodbye, he was there. Larger than life, eyes boring into hers. He captured her chin in one hand and tilted her face up to him. He bent and brushed the softest hint of a kiss across her lips.

"Goodnight, Ali."

A second later he was gone.

Chapter 9

Evan groaned as he climbed out of his SUV Wednesday night. The humid air surrounded and clung to him, making him feel like he'd stepped out of his air conditioned vehicle and straight into a sauna. A car honked in the distance, and the bass of a speaker blasted as a pick-up truck drove by. Hell. What he wouldn't give for a moment's peace and quiet. His entire body was sore from the PT and drills they'd conducted on base today. He'd lifted weights with his SEAL team that morning, nothing too out of the ordinary, and they'd drilled in combat that afternoon.

Evan had sparred with Patrick and Christopher, one right after the other, leaving his body on edge and exhausted. The punches and jabs they'd exchanged left him aching and sore, and although he'd briefly gotten one up on Christopher, taking him to the floor, he'd fought back twice as hard. Those guys were massive, and although Evan could hold his own with any of the men on his team, he felt the deep ache in his muscles from all that exertion. He sure as hell hoped they were as sore as him. As the youngest guy on his SEAL team, wasn't he supposed to have the advantage?

Still, even at twenty-seven, some days he already felt like he was too old for this. What had been fun and exciting years ago wore him down some days now. The Navy had been his life, his career, his everything. Now that he was older, he was starting to see there were some other things he needed. A wife. Kids of his own. A family.

Tomorrow he'd get in a long run, clearing his head, and letting his body recover. He wasn't sure what had him all out of sorts lately, but he was ready for something to change. Thank fuck they weren't doing the same drills again tomorrow. His mind and body both needed a break.

Everyone had been on edge today on base, a sizzle electrifying the air. There had been an urgency underlying the day-to-day regimen he and his team had grown accustomed to. They'd been back from their last deployment for only a couple of weeks, but it was quiet—too quiet. Something was on the horizon. He could feel it in his gut.

Their CO hadn't given word of any impending ops, but Evan could sense a stir in the air on base. A change in his commander's focus. Something big was coming.

His team was trained to be ready at all times. They were at the government's beck and call twenty-four/seven, whether they liked it or not. Such was the life of a SEAL. They'd rapidly deploy when called up, leaving within hours, and he was just waiting for the word. Years in the military had left him attuned to his surroundings, and with the silent hush-hush energy on base today, he knew, without a doubt, they'd be on a transport sooner rather than later.

Once again he'd be whisked off on a mission. Just like that.

That hadn't fared so well for Patrick last time, as the team had been sent off right after the incident with Rebecca's stalker. His teammate had been furious at wheels-up, livid over the entire confrontation with the man stalking Rebecca and subsequent fight he'd had with her. He'd never seen a man look so angry and shattered at the same time.

The entire SEAL team had been watching over Rebecca and her daughter that week. Patrick's asking for help in their protection only solidified how much she meant to him. The team's shipping out in the midst of his personal crisis wasn't ideal, but when Uncle Sam needed you, you went. Luckily their relationship had a strong enough foundation to build on, and now those two were as happy as any couple he'd ever seen.

Maybe someday he'd find that.

The craziness on base sure didn't give him much time to wonder.

He stalked through the dark parking lot of the shopping center. It was already after nine, but that didn't matter to his grumbling stomach. Hours of training followed by a few rounds of pool and beers with the guys had left him famished. The only thing welcoming him at home would be an empty fridge, so it was time to stock up on some necessities.

A swish of long red hair caught his attention as a woman in scrubs climbed out of a car a few spaces ahead of him. She was petite, and even in the low light, there was no mistaking the spun rose-gold shade of that hair. Narrowing his eyes, he saw that it was indeed Alison. What was she doing shopping alone this late at night?

"Alison!"

She jumped a foot in the air, her hand clutched to her chest, and he chastised himself for scaring her. Walking closer, he glanced down at his black tee-shirt and army-green cargos. He looked like he was conducting some kind of night-ops raid out here in the dark. All he needed was his body armor and weapon. Because that wouldn't look too threatening.

"Evan?" she asked, looking relieved to see it was him. Hell. All he needed was to scare her into another asthma attack or something. Did that even trigger them?

Wait a second. Was she trembling?

"Aw, hell, Ali. I didn't mean to scare you." He reached out and stroked her arm, feeling the goose bumps coating her skin. His need to touch and comfort her surpassed all other wants. Suddenly his tiredness and hunger seemed secondary to making sure Alison was okay. He was the type of man to watch out for a woman. To defend and give shelter. Protecting others was engrained in his DNA, and having her startled because of his move didn't sit well with him.

She relaxed as his fingers lightly brushed up and down her arm, reassuring her. Nothing would ever happen to Alison when he was around. Hell if he didn't wish he could tell her that. He'd just about pushed the limit last weekend, brushing her lips with a soft kiss. He could tell she was skittish of getting too close to him. She might as well be wearing a big "Proceed with Caution" sign.

"What are you doing here?" she asked.

"Same as you—grocery shopping."

She raised her eyebrows.

"I didn't mean to scare you," he repeated, reluctantly taking his hand away. Part of him wanted to tuck her into his arms, to hold her close and keep her safe, but that didn't seem appropriate at this exact moment. She still seemed a little wary. Unsure. The way she looked up at him right now killed him.

His eyes drifted over her porcelain skin, green eyes, and rosy lips. She was so delicate compared to his own hard, masculine features. Weak where he was strong. Soft where he was hard. Gentle compared to the warrior in him. His exact opposite.

Her fruity scent once again slammed into him. One of these days he was dying to discover whether all of her skin held that intoxicating aroma. To kiss his way up and down her body. To make her cry out for him as she came.

"I just got off work."

Aaaand back to reality.

"You look cute in scrubs," he said, winking at her. The pale blue v-neck top was modest, but he was so much taller than Alison that he could see the swell of her breasts peeking out from beneath the fabric as he gazed down.

Not that he was looking. *Right.*

Despite the loose, almost baggy fit of the top, she looked just as enticing as when she'd had on that sexy dress the other night. Who knew he'd find scrubs so damn attractive?

Hell.

"And you look cute as Rambo," she muttered, turning around to head toward the store.

"Cute, huh? I'll take it."

He grinned as she walked off in a huff. Damn, she was adorable when she was mad. Two long strides, and he'd nearly caught up with her. He held back a moment, enjoying the way her ass swished back and forth in her scrubs. Those things looked like they were made of the thinnest cotton imaginable. Too bad he didn't have a good reason to haul her into his arms again tonight. He bet that he could feel every curve of hers beneath that soft fabric.

He stifled a groan as he fell into step beside her. "Why are you out here so late by yourself?"

"Late? It's not even nine o'clock."

"It's dark out," he said, an uncomfortable tightness constricting his chest. He didn't like the idea of Alison loading her car full of groceries by herself in the dark parking lot. Or hauling them into her townhouse alone. Some creep could be watching her and follow her home. Hell, Rebecca had a stalker waiting right outside her house. What if someone was scouting Alison's neighborhood? It was a safe area, but an attractive woman all alone at night could draw unwanted attention. She'd be distracted, unpacking her bags from the car. She'd never notice if some asshole was watching her.

Wait. Her townhouse had a garage, right? Well, that was something. It still didn't sit well with him.

"You should go shopping during the day," he insisted.

"I was working," she said, grabbing a basket. Evan took it from her without thinking, following her to the produce section. She selected a pre-packaged salad.

"Is that your lunch for tomorrow?"

"Nope. Dinner."

"No way," he said, taking it from her and shoving it back into the refrigerated section.

"What are you doing?" she asked, looking slightly annoyed. Come to think of it, she looked pretty exhausted. Dark circles that hadn't been there over the weekend were shadowing her eyes. Had she not been sleeping well? Or maybe she was just tired from whatever shift she'd been on. She worked some kind of crazy schedule—a few days on, a few days off. If she had to cram a forty-hour work week into just a few days, those must be some long-ass hours. Something he was more than accustomed to during their ops. Running on a few hours sleep was standard when they were called into action.

"I'm starving. You obviously just got off work at the hospital. I'm cooking us dinner."

"It's nine o'clock at night."

"I think we established that," he said, trying not to smile.

"Look, sorry if I'm being grumpy, but I'm tired."

"Which is exactly why I'm going to cook you dinner," Evan said, a surge of adrenaline rushing through him. Man, had it really been five minutes ago that he was exhausted beyond all belief? Seeing Alison had revived and energized him, sending sparks of electricity and awareness through his entire body. Yeah, maybe his muscles still burned, but hell if he didn't have a second wind that hadn't been there as he'd pulled into the parking lot earlier.

She hesitated, and Evan grabbed her hand, tugging her along. It felt good having her at his side, crazy as that sounded. Something about it just seemed right.

He'd whip them up a quick pasta dinner—maybe find some of those frozen meatballs and a jar of marinara sauce. And wine—they definitely needed a bottle of that. "So, I'm thinking I'll cook at your place," Evan suggested. Some other night he could impress her with *actual* cooking. At his apartment. The woman looked exhausted though, and there was no way he was going to invite her over and then send her driving home alone late at night. Her place it was.

"Hey, if you're really offering to cook me dinner, I won't turn you down."

"Just as friends," Evan added, winking at her. "So don't go trying to rip all my clothes off later on." Alison turned as red as her hair, and he couldn't help but laugh. "Hey, you keep shooting me down when I try to ask you on an actual date."

"Evan—"

"It's cool," he said, cutting her off. "I can do the friend thing for now. But just remember, I'm right here when you change your mind."

"*When* I change my mind?" she asked, her lips quirking at the corners as she fought her smile.

"Bound to happen."

Alison laughed, grinning for the first time all evening. "Are all you SEALs so relentless?"

"It's just part of our charm, baby."

Chapter 10

Alison stretched out on her sofa, a generous glass of Merlot in her hand. The entire evening had been pretty surreal so far, so she was just going with the flow. Maybe she'd wake up in a few minutes from this delicious dream in which a hot Navy SEAL was standing in her kitchen, cooking her dinner after a long day. It had to be too good to be true. Taking another sip of the full-bodied red, she felt her body warm. The second glass was definitely taking the edge off of her stressful day. Angry parents, sick kids, long hours—how could this be only day one back on her shift?

The aroma of the dinner Evan was cooking wafted across the open floor plan of her townhome to where she relaxed in the living room, and she smiled as she saw him shuffling around in her kitchen. His broad shoulders and muscular chest looked oh-so-tempting from here. Maybe she *shouldn't* keep enjoying this second glass of wine. At the moment, he looked positively scrumptious. Almost enough to make her forget that she didn't date younger men.

She could get used to a man cooking for her. Bringing her a glass of wine. Helping her with the groceries. So what if it was the middle of the week, late at night, and she had to be back at work at seven in the morning. This was pure heaven.

After a twelve-hour shift and two hours of unscheduled overtime, she'd finally left the hospital feeling exhausted and frazzled. Wiped out after her first day back. Swinging by the grocery store to grab a quick meal had seemed like the best possible option for the evening. *That, and lots of chocolate.* She'd been so wrapped up in her own thoughts that she somehow hadn't even noticed the two hundred plus pounds of solid muscle heading her way. Huh. Like most women wouldn't notice a Navy SEAL headed straight for them.

Evan had nearly scared her to death in the parking lot. She'd jumped a mile high after he'd called out to her. After the recent incident with Rebecca's stalker in her not-so-distant-memory, having a massive man dressed in dark clothes address her while she was out alone at night had sent shock and fear quaking right through her. The fact that Rebecca's stalker was in jail didn't completely settle her nerves—it just proved there were assholes like him out there. Luckily, she'd realized a moment later that it was Evan.

But still.

In those few seconds that it took her mind to play catch up with her body, she was frozen. Literally trembling in fright.

Evan realized he'd scared her, too. He'd been so

sweet, gently caressing her arm as they'd stood there. Reassuring her. For a guy with such a macho, bad-ass career, he was pretty damn gentle when he wanted to be. When he was with her. Part of her had wanted to wrap her arms around his chest, hugging him tightly and feeling his solid warmth and muscular strength. Inhaling his scent.

But that would've been entirely inappropriate. Damn her sudden urges to only date men with husband potential. Flings were fun, easy. Evan was fun. And more tempting than she'd originally thought when they'd first met.

Still, when Evan had offered to cook dinner for her, she was too tired to argue. Too surprised to put up any sort of fight. Maybe there were a million reasons why she should've turned him down—the first of which being that he seemed *very much* into her. And try as she might, she was attracted to him. Maybe they could be two people who just had dinner together sometimes. Friends did that, right? The fact that she'd seen Evan more in the past few weeks than she'd seen other friends all summer didn't mean anything.

She let her eyes drift shut for a minute as she relaxed back into the cushions. Her hot shower followed by a glass of wine was doing her in. The garlic and marinara scent of the spaghetti sauce permeated the room and made her mouth water. Maybe if she just closed her eyes for a minute, dinner would be ready….

She must've actually fallen asleep, because the next thing she knew, Evan was softly rustling her, trying to wake her up. She met his intense blue gaze, noticed the way his large frame crouched down beside her, and smiled. God, he was beautiful for a man. Handsome face, brilliant blue eyes…smoking hot body. She felt heat rising to her cheeks and was thankful she hadn't uttered any of that aloud.

Maybe she should be embarrassed that she'd fallen asleep on her sofa while she had company over, but this was Evan. Things were easy with him. If he were a man she was trying to impress, she'd have been in the kitchen with him, flirting and sashaying around. But with Evan? She'd felt comfortable enough to fall asleep in her living room.

"Hey, Ali," he said, his voice low. It soothed her just hearing it. The timbre was deep, comforting. The way his words washed over her reminded her of warm caramel. It was rich. Decadent. And she liked the way he called her Ali when he was being sweet and gentle with her. The rest of the time he always said Alison, but he'd called her Ali when she'd had her asthma attack and when he'd comforted her in the parking lot tonight. Did he even realize it?

For a brief moment, she wondered what he'd call her if they went to bed together. If he kissed her, teased and caressed her body, would he still call her the nickname he'd made up? Would he call her Alison or some other name reserved for intimate lovers? He *had* called her baby a few times, but that was more jokingly, like he'd been trying to lay on the charm.

No sense in even wondering how he'd address her if they ever ended up tangled in the sheets, because that was never *ever* going to happen. But still….

"Dinner's ready," he said, eyeing her closely.

She yawned. Stretched languorously. "Sorry I fell asleep."

"No problem." His eyes lit up with his smile. "You

had a busy day."

"Yeah. You could say that."

He took her hand and helped her to her feet. "I had to spar with Patrick and Christopher all afternoon. Busy doesn't even begin to cover it."

"I had to treat a pediatric burn victim."

His face darkened. "You win."

They walked over to the kitchen table, and Alison sank into a chair as Evan insisted he'd get her some food. He seemed proud of himself for cooking her a decent meal, so she went with it. That and the fact that she'd just woken up—carrying a plate of steaming hot spaghetti over to the table didn't seem like the best move at the moment. "That's a contest I never want to win," she said with a sigh. "It's just too damn sad."

"I've seen a lot in my years in the Navy—but nothing is as hard as looking at an injured child. It eats me up inside to deal with monsters who'd hurt innocent women and children."

Alison glanced up at Evan, seeing the anger cross his expression. He'd probably seen more than most guys his age. Heck, he'd probably seen a lot more than her.

She brushed some of her hair back from her face, taking a bite of the food. It tasted delicious, the Italian meatballs pairing perfectly with the spicy sauce. So what if it wasn't completely from scratch. It was much better than the quick salad she'd intended to have.

She wondered how well Evan really knew Rebecca or her daughter. The whole team seemed to hold an affectionate spot in their hearts for the two of them—either because they'd all come together to protect

Rebecca during the stalker incident or because she'd won over their hardened SEAL team member. Patrick's nickname was "Ice," after all. *Which reminded her….*

"Rebecca said Patrick's nickname is Ice. Do you have some kind of crazy name, too?"

"Crazy?" His eyes sparked as he watched her.

"You know. Some macho, made-up SEAL name no one else knows about."

Evan laughed, a deep hearty sound. It sounded loud in her normally quiet townhome, and Alison realized that she liked it. She liked his presence here, too, she had to admit to herself. Maybe even a little bit too much. He filled up physical space with his large frame, but his personality warmed her home as well. He was friendly and teasing. Caring. Tough. There were so many different sides to him, and a part of Alison longed to see all of them. To know *all* of Evan.

"All the guys end up with a nickname—either in BUD/S or sometime soon after when they become part of a SEAL team. It's not exactly top secret stuff, though."

Alison watched him, enjoying the grin on his handsome face. He had a bit of a five-o'clock-shadow tonight—not very prominent, since he had blond hair. The bit of scruff did manage to make him look older though. She decided she liked it. He stretched, gripping his muscular hands together as he flexed those massive arms. Evan was so, *sooo* the exact opposite of the last guy she'd dated. How had she ever thought she'd be interested in a buttoned-up accountant type?

Evan was daring and adventurous. His very job

was one most men could never hope to achieve. She wasn't sure how many Navy SEALs there were, but it couldn't have been a heck of a lot. Those tests were grueling—she knew that much. She expected guys like him to be cocky, arrogant. Maybe some of them were, she thought, recalling Brent. Evan was confident, yes, but not in an obnoxious way. He was comfortable in his own skin. Friendly. Although she had no doubt he would fight to the death to protect those he cared about, he didn't go around flaunting his power or strength. It just was.

Starting anything with Evan would be a bad, bad idea. But how many men would cook dinner for a woman they barely knew when she'd already said they were just friends? Either he was just an extremely nice guy or else extremely confident that he'd somehow convince her to change her mind. Licks of heat coursed through her at the idea, and she thought of the many, *many* ways Evan could touch and caress her with those large hands. She bit her lip as she watched him.

"I'd give my left arm to know what you're thinking right now," Evan admitted, his voice rough.

"Nothing." She couldn't hide her smile.

"You're trouble." Evan smirked. His blue eyes danced as she met his gaze.

"Tell me about this nickname," she said, taking a sip of her wine.

"Oh, it's nothing too cool. The guys call me 'Flip.'"

"Flip?"

"Yeah. I was a swimmer when I was younger—lifeguard, too. You couldn't keep me out of the water. Anyway, one weekend before BUD/S we all went cliff diving."

"Cliff diving?"

"Yeah, out in California. It's kind of a daredevil, thrill-seeker type of thing. Mostly for the young and foolish. We'd hike up these massive cliffs out there— the view was pretty spectacular. Then we'd line up, jump off the edge, and land in the ocean."

She looked at him in horror, and he grinned. "Not an adrenaline junkie, huh?"

"Definitely not."

"Yeah, it might not be good with your asthma anyway."

"Evan—"

"Yeah, yeah. Back to my story. Cliff diving is dangerous, but that's part of the fun. The rush. I'm not dumb enough to try it anymore, but hell, I was young then. And don't get me wrong—the thrill of it was exhilarating. Some of the other guys jumped off, shouting and howling as they landed in the water below. I decided that I had to show them up. Why jump off a cliff when I could dive or do some trick?"

"You did a flip."

"I somersaulted through the air. One of the craziest things I've ever done, because I could've hit my head on the rocks."

"You could've hit your entire body on the rocks— splat."

"Yeah, guess so."

At least he had the decency to look a little sheepish. "We see injuries in the hospital all the time from people being reckless. That's dangerous, Evan."

He chuffed out a laugh. "I'm a Navy SEAL, Ali. My entire career is dangerous."

She frowned as his words washed over her. He

was right. Cliff diving was probably one of the least dangerous things he'd done in his lifetime. Those guys deployed to God-knows-where, fighting dangerous enemies, getting right in the line of fire. She didn't even know what he did—couldn't— because it was so highly classified. Fighting with drug lords, terrorists, and insurgents was probably par for the course in the line of duty.

The idea of Evan in harm's way didn't sit well with her.

"Are you worried about me?" he asked, cocking his head.

"Well, yeah." Her stomach flipped as she met his gaze. Butterflies that hadn't been there earlier let loose when he looked at her that way. He reached across the table and clasped her hand, his thumb running over her knuckles. Shockwaves rocked through her at his gentle touch. His hand looked so large holding her own, but somehow it was gentle. Reassuring.

She swallowed nervously, sparks sizzling through her entire body. For a moment, she imagined those hands running all over her heated skin. Touching her. Caressing her. Kneading her breasts. Trailing across her stomach as they went lower….

"Don't be," Evan said, flashing an easy grin. She snapped out of her daze, pulling her hand back before she did anything she'd really regret. "It's dangerous, yes, but we're well trained. That's why I'm so exhausted that I can barely move tonight. We train hard and fight harder."

"And then you came over and fixed me dinner," she said, her voice soft.

He met her gaze. "I like you."

She swallowed nervously. His words were so right, but that didn't negate the fact that he was all wrong. "Evan, thanks for making us dinner, but I think you should go." She felt pinpricks of tears and abruptly stood, dropping her napkin onto the table. "It just wouldn't work between us." She wouldn't let herself date another man who she had no future with. The fact that she was already developing feelings for Evan just showed that she needed to end whatever this was. Now.

"Ali," Evan said, his voice gruff.

She was already exiting the kitchen, crossing through the living room. Her mind whirled from the wine, the late hour, and the heat that had been coursing through her ever since Evan had taken her hand at dinner. The pad of his thumb skimming ever-so-slightly over her knuckles had practically made her shiver in delight. Why did his touch always feel so damn good?

Evan was hot on her heels, easily catching up to her with his long strides. She felt a tightness constricting her chest. They reached the door, his large frame towering behind hers. How ironic that she'd initially been frightened of him in the parking lot. In many ways, she'd never felt so safe or at ease as when she was with Evan. He'd never let anything hurt her. The problem was, who would protect her from *him?* There was no way she could survive another catastrophic failure of a relationship. No way her heart could heal from another hurt like that.

As she reached for the doorknob, Evan caught her hand. Warmth spread through her where his large fingers encircled her wrist. She glanced up at him, confused, and her lips parted.

"Give me a chance," he commanded, his voice low. He released her wrist and brushed a strand of hair back from her face. The heat from his fingertips left a trail of warmth across her skin. "Let me take you out this weekend. On an actual date."

"We can't."

He took a step closer as she stepped back, and he rested his large hands above her on the door, effectively caging her in. His broad chest was inches away, his muscular arms trapping her. He was tall and strong. Virile. The scent of him surrounded her, made her dizzy with want and desire. She tilted her head up to look into those searing blue eyes. They searched hers, penetrated her thoughts, seemed to know all of her secrets.

"Because we're just friends," he said.

He ducked his head lower, and she tried desperately to play it cool, to act unaffected and blasé, but her body betrayed her. Her nipples tightened under her thin top. Her breathing hitched. Heat began to pool in her core.

"Yes," she whispered.

"Because I'm too young for you," he said softly, inching closer to her still. Warmth washed over her skin, and she was certain she was about to spontaneously combust. Flames licked through her body, racing faster and faster until her whole body was alight with awareness. Heat coiled in her abdomen, spiraling down until arousal dampened her panties and she ached for his touch. She couldn't move from where he'd trapped her against the door. Couldn't run from him.

Part of her didn't want to.

"Yes," she breathed.

Slowly, seductively, like he knew she wouldn't be able to resist, his mouth moved inches away from hers. Their heat intermingled; for a moment, she wasn't sure where she stopped and Evan began. She felt her intake of breath as her heart pounded wildly in her chest. She shut her eyes. He was close. Too close. Not nearly close enough.

Then his lips brushed against hers. They were soft and gentle. Warm. Full. She let out a small moan of pleasure, and Evan took control of the kiss. His hands still rested above her on the door as he bent his large frame down to kiss her. He'd caged her in, yet the only parts of their bodies that touched were their mouths. His words, his actions, everything he did had her helpless with wanting him.

She longed for more contact, for him to crush his hard body into her. She needed to feel the muscles in his broad chest pressing against her swollen breasts, his thick erection against her belly.

She needed his hands all over her.

She opened her mouth to him, clutching his tee-shirt with shaking fists. His tongue dipped into her mouth, and he tasted of wine and spicy marinara. Of something darker and distinctively male. He kissed her slowly, leisurely, his tongue dancing with hers like he had all the time in the world. Like he could spend all night exploring her mouth. How he had so much damn control she didn't know. It felt like a fire was racing through her body, sparking every last nerve ending in awareness of Evan's presence.

As she trembled against the door, he finally pulled back. The only thing betraying his casual demeanor was the arousal in his blue eyes. They were darker than she'd ever seen. "I need to have you tonight, Ali.

Fuck, I need to make you come, hear you cry out my name, and bury myself so deep inside you that neither of us can tell where I stop and you begin."

Chapter 11

"Yes," she pleaded, finally giving him the answer he was so desperate to hear. His body craved her. He needed to take her to bed, claim her, and make her his own. He needed his name on her lips, his cock deep inside her, and his scent all over her skin. He could kiss and pleasure her all night long. Fuck the early morning training. He'd stay as long as she'd have him, as long as it took for both of them to be thoroughly sated.

"Ali," Evan murmured, bending down and lifting her into his arms. She was small and completely perfect for him. Her lips were swollen, ripe from his kisses. Her cheeks were flushed. And the way she gazed up at him right now? Hell. He'd do just about anything to see her look at him that way every day for the rest of their lives.

He tucked her body against his chest, feeling the rapid rise and fall of her breath. The way her breasts rose and fell was driving him crazy. He was dying to tear off that top and see how she looked in her bra and panties. How she looked wearing absolutely nothing at all.

He carried her down the hallway as she wound her arms around his neck. "I need you," she whimpered.

"You have me." He kissed her again, hard, promising her of all that was to come. This woman was fucking perfect for him, and he wasn't even sure if she realized it yet.

Stepping into her bedroom, he made swift work of removing her top. He'd just about damn near taken her right against her front door a few minutes ago, and he wanted—needed—her spread out on her bed for him. He needed to explore every single inch of her gorgeous body, to caress and kiss every smooth curve, and no way was that happening in her front hall.

He needed to take his time, driving his woman absolutely wild with pleasure. *His woman.* She wasn't his, but hell if he didn't intend to change that before the night was over. He'd never wanted someone so badly before.

Evan grew even harder as he took in her emerald satiny bra. It made her eyes even greener and contrasted beautifully against her porcelain skin. "You are so goddamn gorgeous," he said in a low voice. He palmed her breasts through the satin as he ducked lower for another searing kiss. Kneading and caressing her swollen breasts, he ran his thumbs over her nipples as they peaked beneath his touch. She was so damn responsive. So sexy and utterly irresistible. His cocked throbbed as he gently squeezed her perfect tits.

His hands slid to the waistband of the leggings she'd put on after her shower. He briefly grabbed her ass through the soft fabric, pulling her closer to him. Fuck yes, he could feel all her curves through these. His fingertips trailed over the swell of her bottom as he enjoyed grinding himself against her core. He could feel the heat from her center and longed to sink his throbbing cock deep inside that tight heaven.

Soon enough he would have her. Make her his.

First, he needed to drive Ali completely out of her mind.

He slipped his fingers in the waistband of her leggings. They were going this instant.

He peeled them down her legs, helping her step out of them. Emerald bikini-style panties greeted him, and he groaned. Did Ali always wear matching lingerie? The woman looked as gorgeous as some sexy lingerie model. Hell.

He stood and kissed her, enjoying the mewling sounds she made as he deepened the kiss. Lowering his lips to her neck, he inhaled her citrusy scent. He nibbled on her tender flesh, enjoying the way she arched against him, her breasts pressing against his chest. Unclasping her bra, he sank lower, taking first one breast and then another into his mouth. She was small but perfect, with light, dusty nipples that stood out against her fair skin. He licked and teased her with his tongue, pulling one taut bud into his mouth until she gasped and clutched onto his shoulders for support.

She tasted fragrant and sweet, like some type of exotic flower made only for him. He could spend all night worshipping her breasts. Sucking, licking, and kissing them while she made those sexy-as-hell little sounds.

And the way she clung to him as he laved attention on her breasts? He was like a man starved for more.

Never mind that he was still fully dressed, Evan couldn't go another second without seeing Alison completely naked before him. Sliding his fingers into the waistband of her satin panties, he felt her tremble.

"Are you okay, baby?" His voice sounded like gravel.

"Don't stop," she pleaded.

Hell no. The only thing that could stop him was her saying the word, and thank fuck she was begging him to continue. He slowly slid the panties down her shapely legs and…fuck. She was completely bare down below. He'd expected to find strawberry blonde curls, but she was smooth. Soft. Irresistible.

He lifted her onto the bed and hauled her to the edge before she could say a word, ducking down to taste all her sweetness. She was wet, already so damn ready for him, and he growled as desire surged through him.

Evan slung her slender legs up over his shoulders as he bent closer, inhaling the sweet scent of her arousal. His broad shoulders spread her legs wide, putting her fully on display to him, and he couldn't wait to taste her. To feel her flutter against his mouth and tongue as he made her come.

Alison gasped and tried to rise up onto her elbows to watch him, but he gently pressed down on her flat stomach, murmuring, "Easy, baby. I got you."

He grew uncomfortably hard as he kissed her, feeling her bare flesh against his mouth. Her soft skin against his lips was like heaven. It was sexier than hell. He slowly licked his way up her seam while she moaned beneath him, and he tasted her sweet juices, trying not to groan with pleasure. He'd go down on this woman every fucking day to taste that sweetness. To hear her cries of pleasure as he brought her to ecstasy again and again.

He slid his tongue through her folds, eagerly teasing and caressing her. She whimpered as he continued his erotic kiss, and he moved higher until her reached her clit. As he licked her with tiny ministrations, she gasped and arched up off the bed, crying out for him. Holding her hips firmly in place, he continued to drive her crazy. Licking. Teasing. Urging her higher and higher.

She was at his complete mercy.

Or maybe it was him that bent to her will.

He was down for the count. Lost to everything but Alison. There was nothing that could stop him from pleasuring her until she screamed out his name in ecstasy. Nothing he wouldn't do for her.

Sucking her clit into his mouth, he gently slid two fingers inside her wet heat. Her arousal coated his fingers, and it was the sexiest fucking thing he'd ever felt. She was drenched for him. What it would feel like to slide his cock inside he could barely even begin to imagine.

He softly thrust his hand in and out, listening to her little moans of pleasure. She clamped down around him, and he groaned. She was so damn tight.

"Oh, God, Evan," she gasped, grasping his head with shaking hands.

He crooked his fingers, touching that secret spot inside, and she nearly came undone.

Flicking his tongue faster over her clit, he didn't let up as she began to move her hips toward him. She tightened her grip on his head, her cries growing louder. She was getting closer and closer, and as he thrust his fingers in and out of her velvety, silken walls, she finally screamed and came undone, wildly bucking against him as he sucked every last ounce of pleasure from her.

Chapter 12

Alison gasped as the aftershocks from her orgasm coursed through her. Her legs were strewn carelessly over Evan's broad shoulders. Her sex fluttered against Evan's sexy-as-hell mouth, her inner walls still spasming around his thick fingers. Slowly, she floated back down to earth, finally returning from the mind-spinning heights that Evan had taken her to. *Oh my God.* Whatever he'd just done with his tongue, lips, and fingers had sent her skyrocketing out of this world. She'd never, *ever*, come that hard before. Flown that high. And all he'd done was pleasure her with his mouth. Holy hell.

Evan raised his head from between her legs and sent her a cocky grin. Her heart stuttered as she watched him. The man was massive, a powerful, trained SEAL, and he was bent before her like she was some sort of goddess he was worshipping. He kissed her inner thighs, slowly unhooking her legs from his shoulders. Alison was grateful she was lying down. There's no way she'd be able to stand after an earth-shattering explosion like that.

His blue eyes smoldered as they bore into hers, and she could see he'd been equally aroused by pleasuring her. His erection strained against his pants as he stood. Well damn.

He crawled over her body, tenderly planting kissing up her abdomen, before pulling her to the center of the bed along with him. Waves of emotions she couldn't even begin to explain rolled over her. Part of her wanted to curl up into his arms and never leave, while another part of her wanted to run for the door and never return.

Tears filled her eyes. It was almost too much, too good.

Searching her gaze, Evan pulled her to his side. His hands felt hot on her skin, and one trailed down her back, the other cupping her bottom. He was still fully clothed, somehow managing to look dark and dangerous here in her bedroom. How was it that he'd managed to see her completely nude, to kiss her so intimately, and she hadn't so much as seen his six-pack abs? No doubt he had walls of muscle beneath that black tee-shirt he wore. Yet he was as concealed from her as she was exposed to him.

"Are you okay, baby?"

"Yeah, I'm fine. I was just…overwhelmed for a moment," she said, fanning her eyes. Seriously, *who did that?* Maybe she'd stand up and swoon next. Evan was making her feel all sorts of things she'd never expected. Never wanted.

"Shhh, I've got you," he said, pulling her against his muscular chest. She closed her eyes, burying her head into the crook of his shoulder. Her body fit so perfectly into his. He felt so solid and real beside her. And she had to stop things before they went any further. He was probably expecting them to go all night. That's what guys like Evan wanted, right? A woman to have fun with in bed, who'd love nothing more than to spend the night with a Navy SEAL? Maybe he'd have her for more than a night, but guys like him didn't want to settle down.

She pulled away, wrapping a blanket around her as Evan watched with a puzzled look on his face. She crept away from him, edging to the side of the bed until her feet dropped to the floor and she stood. His searing gaze made her feel like she was still wearing nothing at all. Like he could see right inside her, down to her very soul.

She took a shaky step back, away from the force that was Evan. She could tell the exact moment he realized her intentions, because his face became expressionless. "You want me to go?" he asked, his voice low as he climbed out of bed. He sauntered over yet stopped a few feet away, and her bedroom suddenly felt cold.

"Yeah, I think that's for the best."

"Ali—"

"That was amazing, but this just wouldn't work. We wouldn't work."

He nailed her with a gaze, his lips pressed together. He wasn't buying that bullshit but also didn't look like he would argue the matter further tonight. He was angry. Pissed off.

She hugged the blanket more tightly around herself, and he sighed.

One long step and he was right beside her, facing

her bedroom door while she stared at the bed where they'd just lay. "I would've made love to you all night long, Ali."

Without another word, he was gone.

The emptiness she felt was almost unbearable.

Made love. Not had sex with her. Not fucked her senseless. Evan didn't know the first thing about love though. He was too young to want the same things that she did. She wouldn't let Evan—or any other man—hurt her. No one would use her ever again, promising they were meant to be together forever one minute and then pulling a disappearing act the next.

It was better she broke things off now, before Evan stole her heart.

Uneasiness coursed through her as she turned around, looking out her bedroom door at the empty hallway. She clutched the blanket in shaking hands, a feeling of emptiness inside where minutes ago she'd been filled to the brim with ecstasy.

She had a sinking feeling that Evan had already snagged a small little piece of her heart.

A moment later, she heard her front door quietly close. She knew he wouldn't be back.

***

Evan bit back a curse as he strode to his SUV. He clicked the remote and jumped into the driver's seat, slamming the door shut before he backed out. What the hell had just happened? He'd promised himself to play it cool with Alison, to take things slowly until he knew she was ready for more. Ready for *him*. Dinner had been good. He'd felt her eyes on him the entire time as he'd moved around the small kitchen—they'd practically branded his skin with their intensity.

And five minutes ago? Holy hell.

He'd never wanted a woman so goddamn much before. When he'd knelt before Ali, pleasuring her, lapping up all her sweet juices with his tongue—he'd never been so hard in his life. She was his. He knew she'd felt it, too. She'd let herself be open and vulnerable to him, let him have complete control as he'd taken her pleasure. The look in her eyes after he'd made her cry told him more than her words ever could.

Hell. He hadn't planned to cage her in at the front door after they finished dinner, trapping her between his arms and kissing her as if she were the only thing that mattered to him in the entire world. The way she'd looked up at him with such longing—lips parted, eyes wide, breasts rising and falling with her shallow breaths. All thoughts of leaving had flown out the window.

He'd been careful to hold back—to kiss her slowly, sweetly. Not touching her was practically the hardest damn thing he'd ever done. Had she noticed the way his arms shook while they'd kissed?

His body reacted on the most basic level to her— desire, want, attraction, arousal. He had a clawing, animalistic need to have her. And when he'd given in to those cravings and swept her into his arms? He'd had plans to explore her sumptuous body, kiss her senseless, and make love to her until morning.

The second he'd pulled her against his chest while they lay on her bed, it was like she'd put up a wall. Didn't *wham, bam, thank you ma'am* usually end with the woman upset as the man ran out the door? Ali had looked stone cold as he'd walked out of her room. He'd only left because she wanted him to.

The hell with this.

Evan sure wasn't going to beg a woman to be with him. He could still taste her sweet juices on his tongue, and she'd all but thrown him out the door. He could have a different chick every night if he wanted. So why the hell did this rejection sting in a way he'd never felt before?

He accelerated as he raced down the road, gripping the steering wheel. He had to be up again in a few damn short hours for training, and hell if he was going to waste another minute thinking about Alison.

Chapter 13

"Thanks for coming over to help," Rebecca said Saturday morning, pushing a strand of wavy brown hair from her eyes. Standing there in cut-off jeans and a tank top, she looked like she could pass for a college student rather than a successful lawyer, Alison thought. Get her in a courtroom though, and she'd completely tear you apart.

Alison wished she could be tough-as-nails when need be like her best friend. She was used to taking care of others, helping them. Not tearing people down. She knew Rebecca only did what she had to for her clients, but Alison could use a little of that gumption some days. Like now, for instance, when days later her mind was still swirling with thoughts of Evan. She was angry at herself for letting him get to her the other night, for letting him kiss her and carry her off to her bedroom.

She was livid he'd made her want him so damn

much.

She was mad at herself for making him leave.

She was upset he'd actually gone. Not that she'd given him much of a choice.

"No problem; I have a few days off," Alison said, shoving another box of toys and stuffed animals aside. They'd been hard at work for an hour but barely had anything to show for it. How much stuff did one kid have anyway? Rebecca's house never looked cluttered, but when you cleared off all the shelves lining the family room, it added up to a massive amount of belongings.

Rebecca surveyed the stacks of boxes around her family room and massaged her temples. "I have to clear out everything before the carpet installers get here on Monday. Waiting until the last minute was a bad call, but things have been so crazy busy at work, this is the first chance I've had to get anything done around the house."

Alison walked over to the coffee table and picked up her vanilla latte, taking a sip. The hot liquid seeped down her throat, and she briefly closed her eyes. After three twelve-hour shifts at the hospital, plus a few hours of overtime, she needed all the caffeine she could get. Adding in the sleepless nights she'd had over the past several days, and she felt like she was running strictly on fumes. "Where's Patrick? I figured he'd be over here first thing. We could use some muscle," she joked.

Rebecca and Patrick had been practically joined at the hip all summer long. The man barely let her out of his sight after the stalker incident—not that Alison blamed him. She'd been scared for her friend, too, once the entire story had come out. There was security at Rebecca's office building and the courthouse, but on the weekends? Rebecca and Patrick were always together, their kids not far behind. She'd half-expected to see him already hauling boxes around when she showed up early this morning, the job half-done. Those SEALs didn't joke around about getting up early and getting in their PT. Even though it was just after nine in the morning, this was practically late with the hours they kept.

"He was supposed to help me. Something came up on base, so he's over there with the rest of the team right now. I don't know if he'll be able to come over at all."

"Oh. Right."

"I have a bad feeling they'll be deploying again soon. Patrick's been really tense this past week."

"Do they know ahead of time when they're leaving?"

"It depends, I guess. They don't usually go into base on Saturdays though. I wouldn't be surprised if he was gone by next week."

"Next week?" Alison paused, her coffee cup halfway to her lips. She'd just seen Evan…what…three days ago? He hadn't mentioned he was leaving. That the team was *deploying* to what was likely some dangerous warzone. He'd kissed her until she was breathless and gotten more than intimately acquainted with her. He'd made her come for God's sake. How could he not mention that he'd be leaving soon?

"He'll be fine."

"Who?"

"Patrick. Didn't you just ask about him?" Rebecca tilted her head, eyeing Alison curiously. Alison could practically see the wheels turning in her best friend's head. And she hadn't even told Rebecca about dinner with Evan on Wednesday—or the life-changing orgasm that followed.

Try as she might, she couldn't get the blond Navy SEAL out of her head. Her mind had been replaying Wednesday night in her bedroom like an endless movie—except it was strictly the highlights reel. Couldn't the man at least be a bad lover or something? Now she had *that* to remember him by as well. And remember was all she would do, because if she ever saw Evan again, she'd be running the other way. He was way too tempting for her self-control.

"Yes, Patrick," she stammered. "Who else would I be talking about?"

Rebecca nailed her with a gaze. Her whip smart lawyer instincts seemed to be calling bullshit on Alison's maneuvering around the subject. Why did Rebecca have to know her so well?

"Well, maybe the Navy SEAL that drove you home the other night for starters," Rebecca teased. "Evan, was it?"

She sighed. "I saw him again the other night."

"Again? You mean after last weekend?"

"He made me dinner on Wednesday."

"What?" Rebecca asked, pausing in the midst of grabbing Abby's stuffed elephant from the armchair. She tossed it back down and turned to face Alison.

"Evan. Made. Me. Dinner." Alison repeated, as patiently as possible.

"He asked you out?"

"No. It's kind of a long story…," Alison said, turning away. She grabbed some throw pillows and a blanket from the sofa and stuffed them into a box.

"...starting with us running into each other in the parking lot and ending with him cooking me dinner in my kitchen. Well no, technically, it ended in my bedroom."

"Sounds promising so far," Rebecca teased.

"I don't know. It wouldn't work," she mumbled.

"Did he stay the night?"

"I told him to leave."

"That bad?"

"That good."

Rebecca laughed. "That's why you're so upset Evan is deploying?"

"I'm not upset," Alison huffed, cramming more stuff into the overflowing box. Honestly, if she couldn't count on her best friend to be on her side, then who could she count on? And was it so much to ask for the man who'd been in her bed to let her know he was leaving on a mission with no idea when he'd return? Or if he'd even return at all?

A chill snaked down her spine. Those guys deployed all the time. She'd known what Rebecca went through each time Patrick had to leave. The reality of the situation began to sink in when she imagined Evan in Patrick's place. He'd leave. Frequently. She'd have no clue where he was, how long he'd be gone, or if he'd ever return. Fan-freaking-tastic.

The way his face had turned to stone as he walked out of her bedroom had left her uneasy for the past several days. He hadn't just been disappointed, it almost seemed like he'd been hurt. Like *she* had somehow hurt him. If he didn't mean anything to her, then why did she care so damn much? And more importantly, if he was just looking for a good time, why would he be offended she wanted him to leave? Those guys had women hanging all over them.

She glanced over to see Rebecca looking at her in disbelief.

"I'm not upset," Alison repeated.

"Uh-huh. And I'm not madly in love with Patrick."

Alison continued packing, ignoring her friend's last statement. "Where's Abby?"

"My parents have her for the weekend. I didn't think my packing up all her toys would go over so well with a four-year-old."

Alison laughed for the first time all morning. "I hear you. Abby's a sweetheart, but you might only have one box of stuff packed by Monday if she were here helping."

"Exactly. Some days it's a wonder I get anything done."

"Want to go out somewhere tonight? Maybe grab a drink?" Alison asked. It was rare that the two of them had any girl time alone. If they met for dinner, Abby usually came along. Alison could use a few drinks and a night out with her best friend, not to mention something to get her mind off of Evan. The sooner she could forget about him, the happier she'd be.

"Absolutely. Want me to swing by and pick you up at seven?"

"Sounds perfect." Maybe the weekend wouldn't be so bad after all.

***

Evan slammed his shot glass down on the table at

Anchors Saturday night, listening to the other guys on his team flirting with the women there. The whiskey burned down his throat, warming his insides. *Too young for her.* Fuck that. If she didn't want him, he'd find another woman who did. First, he needed another couple of drinks to erase the images floating through his mind. Alison, legs splayed over his shoulders as he pleasured her. Fuck if he hadn't ever tasted anything so sweet. The look on her face at the front door as he'd kissed her after dinner. Despite her protests that they were all wrong, she'd clung to him desperately, pulling him closer as he'd swept her mouth with his tongue.

The worst image of all was the one of her clutching the blanket around herself right before he left. Her face had been flushed from the screaming orgasm he'd given her, her hair was tousled and sexier than fuck, and the panic in her eyes had been overwhelming. What the hell was the woman so afraid of? She'd been more than happy to be swept into his arms and carried off to bed. But the moment he'd held her close, tried to be more than just some guy who'd gone down on her, she'd panicked. Froze him out.

Evan had the distinct impression Alison didn't let men into her life very often—not into her townhouse, and definitely not into her bed.

Hell, didn't all women want a man that would hold them close? A man that wanted more than just sex and a one-night-stand? They hadn't even lasted until the sex or one-night part. He'd licked her senseless, loving every fucking second, and she'd practically kicked him out. All that had been missing was her shouting not to let the door hit his ass on the way out.

It just figured that when he'd found a woman he wanted more than one night with, she couldn't handle it. No wonder most of his SEAL team was still single—women were just too damn confusing. A mystery most men would never solve.

Other conversations hummed in the background at Anchors, glasses and beer bottles clinked, and women swarmed around their table. A cute little brunette kept trying to get his attention, but the coy way she bit her lip and gazed at him through hooded eyes did little to tempt him. Mike pulled a sexy blonde onto his lap, and Evan's jaw almost dropped at the extremely low-cut top she was wearing. Why the hell did women think that was attractive? A little cleavage was enticing, but what man would want the entire bar to see his woman's goods on full display?

His mind flashed back to slowly undressing Alison in her bedroom. Kissing her small and supple breasts. She was the type of woman who was completely gorgeous without flaunting it. She didn't dress provocatively, but the way her clothing sexily draped over her curves drove him wild.

Hell. So much for forgetting about the strawberry blonde beauty for the night. He needed something to get her off of his mind, but the ladies trying too hard at Anchors just didn't interest him. At all.

"Hey baby," Brent said, flashing a grin at the brunette who'd been hitting on Evan earlier. She winked but wondered off with some of her girlfriends.

"Shit, what the hell was that about?" Brent muttered.

"She only has eyes for Evan," Christopher joked. "Didn't you see her falling all over him earlier?" He downed the last of his beer and nodded at the waitress walking by, who collected his empty bottle and went off to get another.

"Fuck this," Brent said.

Mike wrapped his arms more tightly around the blonde he was holding and laughed.

"I know Brent's problem," Matthew drawled, a grin spreading across his face as he glanced between the others. "He didn't get laid the other night."

"I told you, you should've gone for that redhead at the party," Mike said as the blonde he was holding excused herself to go to the ladies room. "She was smoking hot and totally into you."

Evan's ears perked up. *The party as in…the barbeque at Patrick's?* Because the only redhead there had been Alison. And there was no way in hell he was letting Brent anywhere near her.

Underneath his bad-boy persona, Brent was a decent guy. His sister had been killed years ago by a jilted ex-boyfriend, and he'd been seething when Rebecca had been in the crosshairs of a stalker a few months ago. Brent would protect anyone in danger, especially a woman, with his own life.

But the rest of the time? The guy was a complete player. He'd been with more women than any of the men on their SEAL team. He channeled his anger and rage over the death of his sister by seeking the pleasure of a woman. And just one woman would never do—that guy needed a constant stream of them. Preferably a new lady every night. No way was Alison going to be his flavor of the week.

"Hell no. She's way too sweet for me. And what the fuck makes you think I didn't get laid?"

They other laughed as Evan bit back a curse. All

that shit about Alison didn't mean a damn thing. Brent wasn't even interested in her, so why the hell was his head pounding and blood boiling after listening to that little exchange?

"You okay?" Patrick asked from beside him.

"I'm fine," Evan ground out.

Patrick raised his eyebrows.

Hell. He was dating Alison's best friend. Women talked. This night was just getting better and better.

"You probably heard I saw Alison again the other night."

"Rebecca might have mentioned it," he commented dryly.

"Let's just say it didn't end well."

"Look, I'm hardly the man to give anyone relationship advice, but Rebecca did say Alison's last boyfriend broke her heart."

Evan raised his eyebrows. He didn't know the what or the how of the circumstances, but his blood heated at the idea of anyone hurting Ali. She deserved more than some prick toying with her feelings. Hell, the woman worked at a hospital taking care of sick kids all day. She'd been worried about him walking her to the door in the rain a few weeks ago because he'd get wet, too. All she did was think about other people. And all that sweetness wrapped up in her sexy little body was almost too much to take.

Christopher started telling a story about some crazy ex-girlfriend of his just as the waitress brought them another round of drinks. Beer bottles and shot glasses covered the table, and their group was growing louder and more boisterous as the night wore on.

Evan downed another shot, the second one going

down more smoothly than the first. Maybe after a few more he'd forget about the clusterfuck this entire week was turning into. He didn't see an easy way out of this situation short of pounding on Alison's door and telling her to give him a fucking chance. There was no way he could show her the kind of man he was if she was going to pull away every time he tried to get close.

He wanted to know more about her past. What exactly had this ex done that had her so spooked about relationships?

"The best part of leaving Coronado was knowing I'd never have to see her again," Christopher continued.

"The babes were smoking hot out there," Brent said. "How bad could she have been?"

Evan's eyes swept the room. The last thing he needed was to listen to Christopher drone on and on about some chick he'd been with years ago. The brunette from earlier was still watching Evan, and he slid his gaze over her body. She was attractive. Not stunning in the way Ali was, but pretty enough. And hell. Was she licking her lips?

What was wrong with him tonight?

Alison wasn't his. Maybe never would be if she had her way. The *too young* for her explanation was obviously just an excuse, because she'd been more than happy to have dinner with him—twice—and let him undress her. The memory of going down on her had him groaning in exasperation. It just figured that the one woman he was slowly becoming addicted to wasn't interested in actually dating him.

He didn't take Ali for a one-night-stand kind of girl. She'd obviously frozen up at the thought of them getting too intimate, going any further, but damn. He hadn't been inside her yet, but he sure didn't kiss every woman the way he had at her front door. He sure didn't pleasure every woman so thoroughly with his mouth and his tongue, with no thought but of bringing her to complete ecstasy. She'd been at his mercy, vulnerable and exposed to him, and the power he'd felt as he seized control of her body, kissing, licking, and sucking until he'd sent her soaring had made him feel about ten feet tall. He'd wanted to roar in approval at the complete way she'd surrendered to him.

But holding her close in bed? Apparently that shit was out of the question.

The brunette across the bar was still watching him, and he rose from the table.

Christopher stopped in the middle of his story and gazed over at the brunette batting her lashes as she watched Evan. "She's hot, buddy."

Patrick narrowed his eyes, but hell if Evan was going to let Alison stop him from enjoying himself. He wasn't planning to go home with the woman, but maybe a little innocent flirting would take the edge off. He wasn't the type of man that needed a woman to nurse his wounds, but hell if he wasn't feeling a little battered and bruised after the cold way Ali had dismissed him the other night.

He was halfway across Anchors in just a few strides, and the brunette left her friends, winding her way through the crowd to meet him. A few male heads turned to watch her as she wove her way through the throngs of people. She was cute. Attractive. But she wasn't Alison. Before he could say anything, the brunette launched herself into his arms, rubbing her breasts against his chest as she kissed him. His hands slid to her hips, and he set her back down. Her kiss did absolutely nothing for him, but she didn't seem to notice or care and asked if he wanted to leave.

Just a few months ago, he probably would've taken her up on that offer. Even if he wasn't feeling it, who would he have been to turn down a good time with a pretty lady? But now? Not a fucking chance.

She brushed up against him again, getting up on her tip toes as she whispered promises for the night into his ear. Was he ever into women this forward before? Jesus. Maybe he should send this chick Brent's way.

She tugged on his earlobe with her teeth, trying to entice him. It had the complete opposite effect, and he pulled away, the pout on her face making him want to groan in exasperation. Maybe he should just call it a night. Not a damn thing had been going his way since he walked in here an hour ago.

Suddenly, a feeling of dread washing over him.

His eyes swept over to the door.

Shit.

Chapter 14

Alison's stomach dropped as she saw Evan kissing the woman in the middle of Anchors. What. The. Hell. For a man who'd acted interested in her, who'd acted almost hurt that she'd brushed him off the other night, he'd sure moved on mighty fast.

Not that she cared. He was obviously not serious about being in a relationship anyway if he kissed multiple women in a week.

Holy crap. Had he taken this woman to bed as well? They sure were acting awfully well-acquainted at the moment. Was that woman tugging on his ear with her teeth?

Alison flushed, anger and hurt coursing through her.

It just figured that the first guy she'd—surprisingly—been interested in and attracted to was about a million different ways wrong for her. Too young. Too carefree. Too frequently deployed. Too macho. Too into sucking face with women he met in bars.

"Alison?" Rebecca asked.

Shoot. They were blocking the doorway, a group of people behind them unable to go in. Well, no time like the present to turn around and leave. There was no way she was staying here after witnessing Evan's public displays of affection in the middle of Anchors.

"Rebecca!" Patrick called out, waving at her from across the bar. Hell. The entire table of SEALs looked over their way. So much for escaping without anyone noticing.

"I have to go," Alison whispered.

"What?" A huge smile spread across Rebecca's face as she beamed at Patrick, but she cocked her head toward Alison.

"I have to go," Alison repeated, louder this time. Tears pricked the corners of her eyes, and she saw Evan trying to untangle himself from the woman he was with.

"But we just got here. And I drove." Patrick was already making his way over to them, and there was no way Alison was going to cry in front of any of Evan's friends. Patrick would certainly give Evan hell for upsetting her, and there was no way she was dealing with the aftermath of that. Better to cut her losses now and get the heck out of there.

Alison turned and bolted from the restaurant, leaving Rebecca standing there looking completely bewildered. She hurried down the block, tears streaming down her cheeks as she edged around slow-moving pedestrians out for the evening. Families and happy couples blocked her path, and she darted around them, moving faster. Farther away. The more distance she put between Evan and her, the better.

Why the hell had she been so stupid? Evan was just like every other man—interested in a little fun for the time being but not interested in anything long term. She should never have let him come over on Wednesday. She already knew last weekend that it wouldn't work between them. But had that stopped her? Not in the slightest. She'd let him into her bed for God's sake. *Shit. Shit. Shit.*

A few people stared at her as she hurried down the block to the boardwalk. She had no idea where she was going and didn't even care. God, she never should have agreed to go to Anchors with Rebecca. They'd had a nice dinner at one of their favorite seafood restaurants, and then Patrick had texted Rebecca to say the team was meeting up for a drink after a tough day. Why Alison thought she could go where Evan most likely would be was beyond her. Obviously she was a glutton for punishment. She should've just taken a cab from the restaurant and left. Or borrowed Rebecca's car—no doubt Patrick would've taken her home.

Finally, she made it to the boardwalk, the ocean breeze whipping her hair around. She felt as crazed as the wind blowing in off the water. The salty air assaulted her senses, and she hastily wiped her eyes. At least out here, with the sun setting, no one would notice her tears. They continued to fall, embarrassment and hurt competing within her. She was the one who'd told Evan to leave the other night, so why did it hurt so much seeing him with another woman tonight? Why was she letting this guy get under her skin?

It stung that she hadn't brought a man to her place

in months, and the first one she finally let in moved on without so much as a backward glance. Nor had he given a second thought to her feelings. Not that he owed her anything, but geez. Rebecca was dating Patrick—certainly Evan would realize that his scene in the bar might get back to her whether he expected to run into her tonight or not. Couldn't he at least have been a little more discreet?

She didn't need this kind of drama in her life.

"Ali!"

She didn't even know that Evan was behind her, but a second later, strong arms wrapped around her, pulling her back. She collided into Evan's solid chest, and he held her there, his front to her back. His warmth and strength surrounded her, the scent that was pure Evan filling her with both comfort and desire. She was supposed to be running from him, upset and angry, so why did his embrace feel so good?

Her body didn't care that her heart felt as fragile as glass, about to be shattered into a million little pieces again. It wanted nothing but Evan.

He rested his chin on her head, his large body holding her close. "Don't cry," he murmured, and it took a second for her to realize that she was shaking in his arms.

"Just leave me alone."

"You ran out of there like the place was on fire."

"You were kissing her," she said, hating the tears that fell. She swatted at them, trying to pull free.

Evan released her but caught her elbow as she began to walk away, turning her to face him. "She kissed me. I sure as hell don't want to be kissing any woman but you."

"It sure didn't look that way," she snapped.

A stray tear ran down her cheek, and she swiped it away, watching as Evan's eyes softened.

"You're the one that told me to leave the other night."

"I just—" she looked away, more tears falling. What did she want?

"I don't want any other woman. I can't get you out of my mind, Ali."

"Evan...."

"I want to finish what we started the other night," he said, his voice rough. It was sexy as hell. His blue eyes sparked with desire, and despite the hurt and her tears, she wanted him. Maybe even because it had hurt to see him with someone else, she wanted him more. The sight of him kissing that other woman had sent jealousy coursing through her entire body. She didn't want Evan's lips on another woman. Didn't want his hands touching someone else.

It was her that needed his tender kisses, his sweet caresses, and those soft lips brushing over her skin. She'd completely surrendered to him the other night, letting him command her body in ways no man ever had before, and she couldn't fathom being that intimate with someone else. Couldn't imagine some other man touching her the way he did.

She didn't want another man; she wanted him.

The air between them grew thick as Evan stepped closer, his focus only on her.

"I need you, Ali."

"This wouldn't work," she pleaded. Her heart was palpitating so quickly, she was certain it was about to pound right out of her chest. Why the hell did she have to want him so damn much?

"I know." He caught her face between two

massive hands and ducked down, planting a kiss on her lips. It was hot, aggressive, and controlling.

"We just can't be together," she gasped.

"I know." Another searing kiss.

"I just can't—"

The rest of the words never came as Evan claimed her mouth with his own. His tongue swept into her mouth, dancing with hers as she surrendered to him. He tasted of whiskey and something else dark and distinctively Evan. His clean scent surrounded her—no aftershave tonight. A hint of sweat clung to his skin, no doubt from chasing her down the block all the way from Anchors. The hint of salt somehow added to his musky appeal, making her want him all that much more. He was all male. Big and strong, commanding, controlling—everything that she wasn't.

Thank God he hadn't just let her run off like a fool.

He backed her against the railing of the boardwalk, and she clung to him, helpless to the feelings of lust and desire washing over her. His massive body towered over hers, and she wanted all of him. Desperately.

"I need you, Ali," he muttered, his voice gravel. "Right now."

His thick erection pressed into her belly, and she felt her panties dampen with her arousal. Damn Evan for making her feel this way. For stirring up desires and longings she never should have with a guy like him.

His hands slid to her bottom, cupping and squeezing, and he pulled her closer as she gasped.

It felt so good pressing up against Evan's solid

frame. To feel how aroused he was for her. He was muscular and solid, pure alpha male wanting to control and dominate. To please and sate. And her body couldn't get enough.

"Where'd you park?" she managed to ask.

"A block away. Come on," he said, tugging on her hand.

"Wait, I should text Rebecca first," she said pulling free of his grasp.

"I told her I'd make sure you got safely home." His eyes were dark with lust and arousal, blue as sapphires under the darkening sky. He took her hand again, lacing his thick fingers between her own, and they hurried down the block to his car.

The sun had already set as they walked into the darkened parking garage. Sounds from the street filtered in—music thumping from stereos, car horns, snippets of conversation. But the inside was completely silent.

They were all alone.

Alison saw Evan's massive SUV parked in a far corner. It was exactly the type of parking spot she'd avoid because it was so secluded, but Evan was six-feet-plus of solid muscle. A Navy SEAL. It wasn't like anyone would mess with him. They walked to the passenger door, right next to the far wall of the garage. Evan clicked the remote to unlock the doors, the *chirp-chirp* echoing throughout the walls of concrete. Alison reached for the handle, but Evan suddenly gripped her hips from behind her, pushing her against the SUV.

"Evan, someone will see us," Alison whispered frantically as his hands slid to her breasts and he ground his erection into her ass.

"I won't let anyone see you."

The gauzy sundress she had on did nothing to conceal her from him. She might as well have been wearing absolutely nothing at all. His hands kneaded and caressed her aching breasts, and his large frame bent over hers, shielding her. Dominating her. He plucked at her nipples, which had peaked beneath the thin material. He teased and tormented her, causing her to gasp and rock back against him.

One muscular hand slid to her thigh, and he teasingly traced upward toward her throbbing center.

"What kind of sexy panties do you have on today?" Evan growled, nipping at her earlobe.

"Evan," she moaned. Her mind was screaming at her that this was a bad idea, but her body just didn't care. Couldn't resist. Evan's touch felt too good. She was too worked up from earlier, adrenaline still coursing through her body. Every touch, every kiss of Evan's was sending her higher, building her up even more. When she finally fell, she'd never be the same.

He grazed her inner thigh with his fingertips, slowly, confidently, finally reaching her center. She was already drenched, aching for him. He slipped his hand inside her panties and cupped her sex. The way his hand rested there, between her silky underwear and bare lips, was driving her absolutely wild. It was possessive and sexy as hell. She was his, whether she wanted to be or not. Evan was once again in complete and utter control.

She sighed softly as he eased his fingers through her wet folds, teasing and caressing her. No other man's touch had ever made her feel this way—so lost, so teetering on the edge, and so completely at his mercy. His fingers fluttered against her, and she nearly lost it right there.

Evan's other large hand squeezed one breast, and she gasped, desire overtaking her. He slid two thick fingers into her molten core, filling and stretching her. Possessing her. She gasped, and slowly, he began pumping them in and out.

"Fuck, baby, you're so wet. Do you want me to make you come?"

"Yes," Alison gasped, helplessly thrusting against him. She needed more. She needed everything.

He lightly bit her neck, sending shivers through her entire body. He owned her—mind, body, and soul. She couldn't move away if she wanted to—her very existence centered on Evan and the exquisite pleasure he was giving her.

His fingers slid upward to her clit, tracing her arousal around the swollen nub. She cried out as shockwaves began to burst through her body. She was about to come any second, unable to hold back from the onslaught of pleasure. "I bet you'll feel so good, baby," Evan murmured huskily into her ear. "I can't wait to be inside you."

His fingers swirled faster and faster, and heat coiled down from her center, spreading through her entire body. The waves of her orgasm began to overtake her, and she was about to be pulled under, helpless to the pleasure Evan sought from her. He pinched her nipple through her flimsy dress and worked his hand in her panties even faster. She glanced down, completely aroused at seeing his large hand touching her so intimately. She was still completely dressed, but Evan was building her higher and higher, commanding her body, just as he'd done in her bed a few days ago.

She hung on the edge of a precipice, moaning Evan's name. She was so lost she didn't even care if anyone could hear her. His thick fingers speared her again, filling her as she clamped down around him. He ground the heel of his palm against her clit, working it against her, and she cried out as she shattered in Evan's arms. He didn't let up, and she helplessly bucked against his hand as she rode out the intense waves of pleasure.

Gasping, she collapsed against his SUV, Evan's hand still cupping her breast, his other hand still inside her. It was hotter than anything she'd experienced before, save for the way Evan had pleasured her the other night with his tongue. Holy hell.

"Fuck me running," Evan muttered. She could feel his rock hard erection pressing up against her bottom as he hunched over her body, shielding her from view. Not that anyone could see them in the dark corner, tucked between the wall and his massive SUV, but she loved that protective instinct in him.

Once again, Evan was fully aroused just from pleasuring her. It must be some macho, alpha male instinct to satisfy a woman so thoroughly, because none of her exes had seemed quite so pleased by that feat. Or seemed quite so determined to send her flying that high. Holy crap.

As she slowly floated back down to earth, gasping for breath, Alison quietly laughed. "How about standing?"

"What?" Evan asked, removing his hand from her panties and softly kissing the back of her neck. A light sheen of sweat coated her skin, and his tongue slowly trailed down the side of her neck, causing her to shiver.

"You said 'fuck me running.'"

Evan chuffed out a laugh. "I'm not fucking you standing here in the parking lot. I'm taking you home with me. Making love to you. And not letting you out of my bed until morning."

Chapter 15

Evan hauled Alison into his arms as they stepped through his front door, holding her lithe body in front of him. He palmed her ass, squeezing it tightly and pulling her against his throbbing erection. Her slender arms wrapped around his neck, and her legs clamped around his waist. Hell. She was clinging to him like she was desperate for him to take her. And hell if he didn't want anything more in the world. He kissed her, tasting the sweetness that was pure Alison. He ground his swollen cock against her core, and she moaned. His bedroom was too damn far away.

He carried her a few feet into the kitchen, hastily setting her down on the counter as he brushed aside the mail. It fell to the floor, but his eyes were too busy feasting on her. Her gorgeous legs dangled over the edge, and he stepped in close, feeling the heat from her sex against his groin.

"Evan," she gasped as he rubbed himself

enticingly against her. Her strawberry blonde hair fell straight around the white sundress she had on. Her breasts rose and fell rapidly, the swells of them looking completely sumptuous as he gazed down at her. She looked gorgeous, like some sort of goddess sent especially for him. And he was ready to partake in everything she offered.

"Hang on, baby." He pulled his wallet from his back pocket, searching for a condom, and felt Alison fumbling with the button on his pants. She finally got it open and slipped a hand inside, gripping his throbbing length through his boxer briefs. "Oh, hell, Ali," he groaned. He ground his teeth against the electricity shooting through him. He would explode if she kept this up.

He let her stroke him for a moment and then reluctantly removed her hand. She started to protest, but he pushed the straps from her sundress to the sides, kissing her bare shoulders. She had a light dusting of freckles over her fair skin, giving her a certain innocence. How ironic since she was a few years older than him—a fact she seemed determined to remind him of nearly every chance she got. He may have been younger than her, but he was in charge tonight.

Her citrusy scent washed over him, and he felt his groin tighten. He tugged the top of her dress down, along with her bra, and her pert breasts spilled over the top. She was small and perfect. Her chest heaved as he kissed his way across. She was sweet. Sexy. He moved slowly, taking his time to explore as he felt her shudder. He sucked a pebbled nipple into his mouth, lightly flicking his tongue back and forth. Alison arched her back and cried out, jutting her breasts further toward him.

He growled in approval and then moved to her other breast, lavishing it with equal attention. He sucked the taut bud until Alison grabbed onto his shoulders, gasping. Hell.

Evan reached beneath her dress, and Ali shifted, allowing him to drag down her white satiny panties. One of these days he wanted to watch her walk around his apartment, wearing nothing but some of that skimpy, sexy lingerie. She had on another matching bra and panties set but had no idea she'd end up at his place tonight. What would she wear if they actually planned a hot night together?

He gripped Alison's hips, pulling her to the very edge of the counter. "Evan," she whimpered.

"Lean back," he commanded, his voice rough. She did as he asked, resting on her elbows so she could watch him. Her rosy mouth parted, her cheeks flushed, and her long hair cascaded down behind her. He longed to wrap it around his fist, pull her head toward him, and sink his rock-hard erection into her perfect little mouth, letting her suck him until he went crazy.

First things first.

He was going to drive his woman completely senseless.

He tossed her legs over his shoulders, and she was once again completely spread open for him. He could smell the sweet scent of her arousal, and his mouth watered as he ducked closer to kiss her core. She trembled as he hovered right above her sex, ready to consume her. He would do this every single night for this woman. She didn't even realize how lost she made him. How completely enraptured he was whenever she was near.

He teased and licked her, thoroughly exploring all of her folds with his tongue while she writhed on the counter. She was soft, wet, and completely swollen, dripping with arousal. Lapping up her juices was like enjoying the most succulent nectar. He'd never, ever have enough of the taste of Alison on his tongue. Of the feel of her drenched folds against his lips. He sucked her clit into his mouth, softly working it as he drove her higher and higher. Her breathing hitched, and she arched back, crying out his name as she exploded for him, fluttering against his mouth and tongue.

Her hips bucked against his mouth as she threw her head back in ecstasy. He softly kissed her sex as she rode out her orgasm, nearly drunk on his desire for her.

She was bare. Dripping wet for him. Beautiful.

Fuck.

There was nothing as goddamn sexy as the way Alison came for him. The way she allowed him to give her pleasure made him harder than steel. Waves of possessiveness washed over him. Alison was *his*. He didn't want any other man kissing or touching her. Caressing her. Pleasuring her.

He was going to claim her and make her his own. He'd sink so deeply inside her tight channel that she'd be ruined for any other man. He'd already had her tonight with his fingers and tongue. Now he needed his throbbing cock deep inside her core, filling her, branding her as his own.

Evan stood, gripping her shaking legs in his hands. "I've got you, baby," he murmured.

"Take me to bed, Evan. I need you."

He collected her against his chest and strode down the hall, gently placing her onto the king-sized mattress. He hadn't brought a woman here before, either into his apartment or his bed, preferring instead to spend the night at their place. Easier to leave in the morning.

But with Alison?

He wanted it all.

She quickly removed her bunched-up dress, lifting it above her head as he whipped off his shirt and pants. He sheathed himself and then crawled onto the bed, prowling over her body. The way she gazed up at him slayed him. It was helpless, desperate, and as nearly as far gone in lust and desire as him.

His cock brushed up against her sex, and he teased her folds, pacing himself. She was so wet for him. So ready. Alison took his throbbing erection into her hand and guided him to her entrance. He eased inside, the head of his cock just pushing into her velvety heat. She was so tight. He tried to go slow, gentle, until it was impossible to hold back.

He inched in further, finally seating himself deep inside, knowing he'd found heaven right here.

***

Alison gasped as Evan entered her. His thick erection slowly sank inside her, inch-by-inch, until he filled her completely. She'd been wet and ready for him, desperate for him to fill and claim her as his own. He bottomed out and held completely still, holding his muscular body above hers, letting Alison get used to him. Evan was so large, it took a moment to adjust to his size. He filled and stretched her in a way nothing ever had before, as if he were made for her alone. She moaned and rocked against him, the exquisite pressure almost too much to bear.

He thrust into her slowly, sweetly, sliding his forearms beneath her back as he rested his weight on his elbows. His blue gaze bore into hers, trapping her more than his large body atop hers ever could. She was completely lost to him, and they moved as one, his muscular biceps bunching up beside her with each thrust. She felt her body humming again, building toward another explosion as Evan stroked her deep inside. Her walls began to clamp down around him, and he began moving faster, the base of his penis rubbing against her swollen clit.

She cried out, unable to control the pace of their lovemaking as Evan powerfully consumed her, bringing her to the precipice once more. She dug her fingernails into his shoulders and wrapped her legs around his waist, locking her ankles together as she hung on. He pumped into her faster, harder, pushing her further toward the edge. He pulled nearly all the way out and slammed into her once more as she finally detonated, screaming in ecstasy. He continued bucking into her as she rode the waves of her orgasm, the moment going on and on until she was exhausted beneath him.

Evan impossibly hardened even more and then gave two more powerful thrusts, saying her name as if it were a prayer while he released deep inside her.

He rolled them to the side, hitching her leg up over his hip, his cock still buried within her pulsing walls. Muscular arms wrapped around her, pulling her closer as his entire body curled around hers. She gasped against his neck, burying her head into the crook of his shoulder as he held her. He was in her, wrapped around her—his very scent covered her skin. There was no part of her unaffected, untouched, or unchanged by Evan.

There would be no running away from him tonight. Not now. Not after that life-altering explosion, not with the way their bodies were still joined as one. Maybe things would look different in the light of day, but for the moment, for tonight, she only wanted him.

Chapter 16

Evan awoke, yawning, a feeling of deep satisfaction filling his chest. The sunlight beamed in through the windows, flickering light across his king-sized bed, and he tried to remember the last time he'd slept in past dawn. When was the last time he'd actually been happy to spend the entire night with a woman? Probably...never?

After a shitty few days, he'd finally brought the woman he was crazy about home with him last night. Maybe he'd had to chase her down the damn street, but he'd taken her back to his place. Had her in his own bed. Made love to her until they'd both drifted off to sleep. Smug male satisfaction coursed through him. Hearing Alison scream out his name again and again was the sexiest thing ever. Feeling her inner walls clench around his cock as he took her, made her his own, made him want to roar in approval. Alison was his.

And it wasn't just about the sex—although that had been off-the-charts spectacular. His new favorite thing was exploring her body, making her come and completely shatter in his arms. It was more than just physical though—he cared for her. His heart had nearly exploded out of his chest when he'd seen the hurt expression on her face at Anchors last night. His only thought had been finding her, making things right between them, and then finally making her his.

He'd torn out of there so fast, he was sure the other guys would be ribbing him the rest of the year. The hell if he cared. Patrick would've probably kicked his ass for hurting Alison—and rightfully so. Thank fuck he'd gotten it together enough to go after his woman. And she was his now—he'd thoroughly claimed her last night, pleasured her, and made certain she'd never want another man again.

He reached across the sheets, wondering why her warm little body wasn't tucked into his right now. He'd woken her once in the middle of the night, his cock harder than steel, and they'd sleepily made love before falling asleep in each other's arms again. The way she nestled against him was probably the cutest damn thing he'd ever seen—like she needed him. And not just because he was some tough Navy SEAL— she'd needed Evan the man. And hell if that didn't fill his chest with a kind of pride he couldn't even begin to explain.

Sitting up, he glanced toward the master bathroom. The door was wide open, the room empty. His brow furrowed as he scanned his bedroom. He never, ever slept this late, but then again, he'd never been so wrapped up in a woman before—literally and figuratively. Alison had him by the balls and didn't even know it. He was completely crazy for her.

He climbed out of bed, pulling on a pair of jeans. Not bothering to fully zip them, he sauntered out to the living room. He had no idea what Ali was doing up so early after the night they'd had, but he sure as hell didn't plan to let her stay out here alone. They had a lazy Sunday to spend together, one in which he planned to enjoy getting fully acquainted with her gorgeous body. The hours that had passed since they'd last made love were too many—he needed to have her again. To slake his need and satiate her.

She was the first woman he'd even brought back to his apartment here in Little Creek. When he was younger, he'd take a woman home with him for the night, but over the years, he'd only stayed at the woman's place. It was easier to sneak out in the middle of the night, easier knowing they wouldn't track him down to his apartment looking for more.

The thought of possibly deploying again in the next week or so was almost painful. His chest tightened at the idea of leaving Alison here while he shipped out. Never, ever had he cared about a woman while he was gone. His focus was on the mission. His men. The women he'd been with in the past had always just been a warm body in his bed—there for his pleasure. He'd certainly enjoyed driving them wild, too, but it had all been about immediate sexual gratification for both of them. One woman was easily replaceable with another.

He walked into the empty kitchen. It felt as lonely as the rest of his apartment did at the moment. His eyes fell on the table—completely bare. He was pretty damn certain Ali had left her purse there last night.

Glancing around his living room, a feeling of

uneasiness began to wash over him. What. The. Fuck. She was gone.

***

Alison climbed out of the cab, shoving a handful of bills at the driver. Last night had been an epic mistake. She'd awoken early this morning, Evan's hard body wrapped tightly around hers, and had a brief moment of panic. They hadn't made any promises to each other, hadn't even been out on an actual date, and somehow she'd ended up spending the night at his apartment. In his bed.

She'd untangled herself from his muscular arms, miraculously not waking him, and snuck into the kitchen for a glass of cold water. As she tried to tell herself she was freaking out over nothing, she'd collected the pile of mail they'd knocked to the floor last night, tossing it onto the counter and accidentally bumping the answering machine. As images of Evan making her come on his countertop flooded her mind, his mouth on her in the most intimate way imaginable, a woman's sexy voice purred on the recording, asking him to call her. Because she'd had a great time with him on Thursday night.

Thursday night. As in one night after he'd made dinner for her and hauled her off to her bedroom.

Hot tears streamed down her cheeks as she opened the front door of her townhouse. What did she expect? She knew he was too young, that guys like him had women hanging all over them. Yet she'd gone ahead and slept with him anyway. She debated calling Rebecca to vent but didn't want to wake her so early on a Sunday. This seemed kind of like a best friend emergency though. Briefly, she debated driving straight there. Pouring her heart out to the one person who'd understand. Then again, Rebecca might be over at Patrick's. Maybe she *should* call.

Her phone beeped with a text message, and her pulse pounded when she saw it was from Evan.

Are you okay? Where'd you go?

Furiously, Alison texted him back.

Check your messages. It sounds like you have plenty of women to keep you busy.

Her phone started ringing a second later, and she pushed the "ignore" button. There was no way in hell she was talking to Evan or letting him chase her down again. She'd been enough of a fool last night to let him convince her that the woman in the bar had been coming onto him—not vice versa. Holy crap. What if she was the one who left the message? She certainly seemed to know Evan pretty well. *Damn it. Damn it. Damn it.*

Alison stormed into her bedroom and changed into her workout clothes. The adrenaline and anger rushing through her were putting her on edge, making her furious. She should probably have something to eat before she went out, but she was too angry to bother. There was certainly no need for coffee when the rage coursing through her had her wide awake and alert. At the moment, she wanted to wring that bastard's neck.

Her phone beeped again, and just before she could haul it clear across her living room, she realized it was a text from her brother:

Coming to VA Beach this week. You up for company?

God, well at least she'd have something to look forward to. If she could convince him to drive down today, she'd have a couple of days off to spend with him before her shift started. Hmmm. She'd give him a call when she returned from her walk. She needed to cool off first, and there was no way she was discussing guy problems with him.

Leaving her phone on the counter, she grabbed a bottle of water and stormed back outside. The sooner she burned off some of this rage seething in her, the happier she'd be. Maybe.

***

Evan pounded his fist on the countertop, anger and frustration pumping through him. What message? What women?

This was ridiculous.

He riffled through the mail on the countertop as if that would give him some sort of clue. It had been scattered all over the floor last night before he'd taken Ali to his bedroom, so she must've picked it up off the floor earlier. He sure didn't see any type of message that would make her go berserk. Not that there even were any other women.

"Hell," he muttered, glancing around his kitchen.

His eyes fell to the answering machine on the counter. He rarely used his landline but pushed the play button just for the hell of it. There sure were no written messages lying around, so what else could she have been talking about? Not a damn thing about this morning was making sense. And Ali storming off again was frustrating the hell out of him.

The answering machine beeped, and the woman purring at him as the message played back had him baffled. *Thursday night?*

He listened to the message all the way to the end, then hit play again. An earlier message began to play first. *"Brent, baby, give me a call...."*

Jesus. Now Brent was giving out Evan's number to his one-night-stands? Good God. He was going to give him hell the next time he saw the guy. Like he wanted a bunch of angry women calling him.

The meaning of Ali's text suddenly dawned on him. She thought he'd been with another woman the other night? For the love of God. If she kept jumping to conclusions, no way in hell would this work between them. He grit his teeth and clamped his eyes shut, his blood pounding. Was she expecting him to chase her all the way over to her townhouse? He'd just tried calling a few minutes ago, and she hadn't answered.

He stalked back into his bedroom. Maybe after a long run his head would be clearer, and he could figure out what the fuck to do next. At the moment, he just didn't feel like dealing with that woman's particular brand of crazy. She freaking drove him insane, usually in the best way possible. But was she going to run every time she freaked out? Or push him away when he got too close?

His sheets were a tangled mess from their night of lovemaking, and Ali's citrusy scent still clung to them. He shut his eyes, trying to get images of her in his bed out of his mind. Weren't women usually all about talking, communicating, and shit? Ali seemed content to cut and run whenever she was feeling uncertain.

Hell.

His eyes fell on a piece of plastic on the ground next to his bed, and he realized Alison's inhaler had fallen out of her purse. "Damn it," he muttered.

Worry snaked through him at the memory of her having an asthma attack a few weeks ago. He'd felt so desperate as he watched her in her kitchen, panic coursing through him even as her breathing slowly returned to normal. As frustrated as he was at the moment, the protective instinct in him flared up. He'd have to head over there sooner than he'd planned.

Abandoning his idea of going on a run, Evan headed toward the bathroom instead. A quick shower, and he'd be on his way.

Chapter 17

Alison gasped for air and sank down to the ground, falling to her hands and knees. The rough cement cut into her palms, and pain shot through her. Speed-walking down the street had been a crazy idea. She'd been madder than hell at Evan, hadn't had anything to eat, and hadn't even brought an inhaler. Rather than dig a spare one out of her medicine cabinet, she'd set out for a walk anyway. Hell-bent on getting her night with Evan out of her mind, she'd stormed down the street huffing with every angry step.

Tears streamed down her cheeks, her chest heaving as she crouched down on all fours, and a woman rushed to her side. She continued wheezing, unable to catch a breath. Someone rubbed her back, and a sheen of sweat began to coat her skin as panic overtook her.

She couldn't breathe.

The world around her began to grow hazy, and

pinpricks of darkness started spotting her vision. She vaguely heard shouts for help and the woman speaking to the 911 dispatcher on the phone. She tried to speak, to tell her she was having an asthma attack, but no words would come without precious air in her lungs.

She was so dizzy, so tired. It seemed easier just to succumb to closing her eyes for a moment.

She uselessly opened her mouth again, but there was nothing. Her chest hurt. Her lungs burned. The world tilted on its axis.

"Alison!" a male voice shouted.

Footsteps came running in her direction. It sounded oddly like her little brother's voice. It couldn't be him. He lived hours away.

"Hang on!" the man said, crouching down beside her. "The ambulance is coming."

The world faded to complete blackness.

***

Evan's gut clenched as he saw the ambulances at the end of Alison's street. He didn't know how the fuck he knew, but he was positive something had happened to her. He screeched to a stop in the middle of the road and jumped out of his SUV, a police officer yelling at him not to leave his vehicle there.

So they'd give him a ticket. Big fucking deal. If Alison was hurt, he'd never forgive himself. His chest constricted as he thought of the time he'd wasted at his apartment this morning. He should've driven after her. Explained everything. And the second he'd found her inhaler? He should have charged out the door after the woman he cared about, not taken some pansy-ass shower to clear his head. It didn't do a damn thing anyway. He was still completely wound up; he still needed a long run to pound out his frustration. And at the moment, he was burning with a need to see Alison.

She'd be okay. She had to be okay.

In the distance, he saw paramedics loading a woman onto a stretcher, an oxygen mask strapped to her face. Strawberry blonde hair swirled like a halo around her head. The relief that coursed through him was a living, breathing thing. She looked paler than usual, but she was moving. Alive. Okay.

He ran to the crowd that had gathered, edging his way through, needing to be closer. His girl *needed* him, and he'd been sulking around at home pissed off that she'd jumped to conclusions. He'd been *inside* of her mere hours ago, and now she was stretched out on a gurney being loaded into an ambulance.

What the hell had happened? If she'd had another asthma attack, her inhaler still in Evan's bedroom, he didn't think he could forgive himself for not rushing over sooner.

Evan ground to a halt as a young guy took hold of her hand, looking white as a ghost.

His heart thundered in his chest.

What the hell?

The guy bent down, whispering something in her ear as he brushed some of her strawberry blonde hair back off her face. He swallowed, his adam's apple bobbing, and took a deep breath, trying to suck down some air as his lungs constricted. Was that…her ex? Patrick said some jackass broke her heart. Evan didn't have a clue how long ago they'd broken up, but they sure looked pretty damn friendly at the moment.

He clenched his fists.

She'd left his bed less than an hour ago. How the fuck had this guy ended up at her side? Jesus. For all he knew she'd run straight back to him. Part of Evan wanted to storm over there and demand an explanation. Then pound the shit out of this guy for being anywhere near Alison. His blood boiled at watching the man's hands on her. Just as he was getting ready to move, his phone buzzed with an incoming call. Holding it in a white-knuckled grip, he glanced at the screen. His CO's name flashed across.

Hell.

There was only one damn reason he'd be calling Evan on a Sunday morning. The op was a go.

"Jenkins," he ground out as he answered the call.

Of all the shitty timing. He spoke quietly into his phone, turning and walking away from the crowd. He handed Alison's inhaler to a nearby police officer and stalked off the way he'd come. His CO relayed the team's wheels-up time, and Evan slid the phone back into his pocket.

Snatching the ticket from his windshield, he climbed back into his SUV, angrily slamming the door behind him. What the fuck had just happened?

He had less than an hour to get his ass in gear and get on base for their briefing. Then he'd be flying the fuck out of Virginia while some other jackass rode to the hospital with the woman he was falling in love with. The woman who'd stormed out on him this morning.

What the hell else could go wrong today?

***

Alison sleepily looked around the hospital room. What the heck had they given her to make her so tired? She'd been on oxygen, been lifted into the ambulance, and then…nothing. Why couldn't she remember what was going on?

Briefly, in her dizziness and in the midst of the confusion earlier, she'd thought she'd seen a tall, blond man walking away. But Evan wouldn't have been there. Would he?

Her eyes swept around the room. Her brother Derek inexplicably stood by the window, tapping out a rapid-fire text on his cell phone. Late afternoon sun beamed in, making his light red hair glow in the light. How long had she been here? And more importantly, what was Derek doing in her hospital room? Rebecca hovered near him, worriedly checking her phone. Only Abby looked perfectly content, sitting in the extra chair and coloring.

When he realized she was awake, Derek raced to her side. "Jesus, Alison, you scared me to death!"

"Derek," she said, reaching out and grabbing his hand. It was solid and reassuring. "What are you doing here?"

"Good to see you, too, sis. I texted you this morning to say I was coming."

"I know—I was going to call you back after my walk. I thought you meant in a few days."

"Surprise," he said with a sheepish grin. "Hope you don't mind me staying. Although it looks like you could use someone to help you out for a few days. Mom and Dad freaked when I called them."

"Alison," Rebecca cried out in relief. She rushed over and bent down to give her a hug. "Why didn't you bring your inhaler on your walk? I just about had a heart attack when Derek called me. Patrick drove me to the hospital like a bat out of hell."

"Long story. Hey, Derek—I don't suppose you could get me a drink?"

"Yeah, sure. Water? Soda?"

"I haven't eaten all day. Maybe some juice to boost my blood sugar."

"Yes, nurse Alison," he said teasingly as he walked away. Little brothers.... The kid was in college but still acted like a sulky teenager sometimes.

"I swear to God, Patrick almost refused to go. I was so freaked out earlier."

"What do you mean?"

"Those guys got called out on some black op. They flew out an hour ago."

"Flew out?" The pain in her chest was immediate and unbearable. Not that she expected to see Evan anytime soon. He'd called after her text this morning but had been radio silent since. Wait, where was her phone?

She frantically looked around the hospital room.

"What's wrong?" Rebecca asked.

"I need my purse."

"Derek went back to your townhouse and got it earlier. You slept for a few hours. Here," she said, handing it over.

Alison tore inside, snatching her phone. Not a single missed call. Nothing.

There wasn't a reason for Evan to call anyway. She'd left this morning without a word. They weren't exclusive; they weren't dating. If he'd had to deploy, why would he give a second thought to her?

Thoughts raced through her mind: Evan making love to her in his bed last night. Evan...with that goddamn message on his answering machine. Evan in harm's way. Evan…not wanting her.

Tears pricked her eyes.

"Hey, they're gonna be fine, sweetie. It scares me to death every time Patrick deploys, but it *is* what they do. They're SEALs. I'm just thankful most of his team's deployments have been so brief. They could get sent out for a year. A week or two away is nothing."

"Evan never mentioned he'd be leaving."

"Hun, those guys can't say anything. They just disappear."

Alison pressed her lips together, holding in the words she knew were about to spill out. Too bad she couldn't shove her hurt and frustration right in there along with them. Of course Evan wouldn't tell her when he left. They weren't together. Someday he'd be kissing some other woman goodbye each time he was sent out. It would be someone else's job to worry about him when he was gone. To hold him when he returned. "Patrick told you." The words bubbled up and sputtered out before she could stop them. Obviously a man would tell his girlfriend he was leaving. Right?

"We're together. Their families obviously know when they're gone."

Alison raised her eyebrows.

"That reminds me. Have you talked to Evan at all today? I thought you guys might be together after the way he chased you down last night."

Alison silently shook her head.

"Patrick sent me a weird text earlier right before they left."

Alison's ears perked up. "Weird? What'd it say?"

Rebecca looked at her phone, reading the message. "Tell Ali the message was for Brent."

Alison's stomach dropped. That woman was calling for Brent? That was why she'd run out of Evan's apartment without so much as a goodbye? Confusion swirled through her mind, her thoughts a jumbled mess. Why the hell did Brent give out Evan's number? Why did she have to accidentally hear that damn message?

Now Evan was gone, and he had no idea how she really felt. How much she really wanted him.

Tears spilled down her cheeks, and Rebecca leaned down and pulled her into a hug. "Oh sweetie, what's wrong?"

Alison shook her head, and Rebecca took a seat beside her on the hospital bed. "Here's Derek with your juice. Start at the beginning, and tell me everything."

Chapter 18

Evan grabbed his gear, strapping on his Kevlar vest and checking his weapons. Christopher was rapidly firing off some schematic info he'd obtained last minute of the building's layout, briefing the rest of the team before they conducted the nighttime raid. They'd nailed down the procedures to breach the facility, but Christopher had hacked into some database, gaining additional specs. Between that and the emails they'd intercepted, they had a damn accurate idea of where the American soldier was being held in captivity. Easy in, easy out, and they'd be on their merry fucking way.

The flight over to the Middle East on the C-17 cargo plane had been hellish. A long ride like that in uncomfortable seats, headphones on to drown out the roaring of the engines, was never exactly luxurious. The worry and anger churning around in Evan's gut topped all that. He'd been so damn relieved to see that Alison was okay and so angry at himself for not chasing after her the second he'd realized she was gone. Then when he'd spotted the young looking guy holding her hand, brushing her hair aside? It sliced through him like a knife.

No wonder she freaked the hell out every time he tried to get close—she still had feelings for an old flame. And fuck if that shit didn't hurt. He'd wanted to pound on the guy, both for hurting Ali in the first place and for being there for her now. Evan sure the hell hadn't been around when she'd needed him. His head ached with all the conflicting thoughts and feelings swirling around. Stuff like that made a man sloppy—dangerous, even, when his head needed to be one hundred percent in the game.

They'd landed after a fourteen-hour flight and hopped in an armored convoy to their forward operating base. A few hours sitting around waiting for nightfall, going over specs, and with not much else to do but think about the clusterfuck of the past twenty-four hours, and Evan felt like absolute hell. Patrick had approached him earlier, saying he'd briefly touched base with Rebecca after landing, but Evan had brushed him off with a cold, "Not interested, Ice."

His SEAL team leader had looked like he wanted to say more, but a remote base in the middle of the goddamn desert was hardly the place to worry about shit back home. And it's not like they could sit around sending messages back and forth all damn day. So what the hell was the point? He had work to do. If his heart felt like it had been ripped from his chest, he had no one but himself to blame.

Evan ground his teeth together, listening to the

layout of the facility they'd infiltrate. Evan's job was to get his men to their coordinates and then get them the hell out of dodge when the shit hit the fan. He'd remain in one of the armored vehicles during the infiltration, ready to drive his team to safety. A brazen ambush like this was bound to be met by unhappy enemy combatants, but hell. What else was new? It was just another day for their SEAL team. How many rapid deployments had they made this year? How many enemies had they engaged with on missions no one would ever know about? He'd damn near lost count.

He glanced around at his team, all assembled near their armored vehicles. The dry, dusty air burned his lungs even as the sun went down, and he took another swig of water from his canteen. It was hotter than hell out here.

Little Creek, VA seemed about a million miles away right now. Fourteen hours in the air, and it felt like they'd landed in a different world. Had it really been only a day or two ago that he'd taken Alison back to his apartment? Made love to her until morning?

That felt like another lifetime.

Pining over a woman seemed downright ridiculous at the moment as the other members of his SEAL team suited up. Trivial at best. He needed his head in the game, not on some woman he'd never have. Hell. Alison was a lot more than some chick he'd banged. She was the type of woman that could make guys like him want to settle down. Raise a family. Get out of the Navy. On their deployment earlier this summer, Patrick had been all bent out of shape over a fight with Rebecca. Now Evan couldn't get Rebecca's gorgeous best friend out of his head? Damn it all to hell.

The other guys were bickering about something, and Evan glanced over in their direction.

"Shit, man, do you need to tuck her in every night, too?" Brent asked sarcastically, coolly eyeing Patrick.

Evan grabbed his HK416 assault rifle, checking to make sure it was loaded and ready. In ten minutes, they'd be rolling out of their forward operating base in the middle-of-nowhere Afghanistan, headed into yet another war-torn town. Evan's blood boiled as Brent continued to argue. If those two didn't stop their yammering, he wouldn't be able to concentrate on navigating through the foreign terrain. He'd pinpointed the precise location, memorized the route, but listening to Brent was getting on his last nerve.

Evan was about ready to start throwing some punches himself if those two didn't shut up.

"Hell," Patrick bit out, slamming the door of their armored vehicle shut. "She's a grown woman. That sure as shit doesn't mean I like leaving her alone."

It was a rare outburst from Patrick, who'd earned the nickname "Ice" for a reason. Calm, cool, and collected was usually the way he rolled. Apparently that applied to every situation except where Rebecca was concerned. Worry creased Patrick's brow.

"She's fine, man," Christopher interrupted. "That asshole's locked up, and Rebecca's a smart woman. She wouldn't put herself in danger. She and Evan's girl will be fine."

"She's not my girl," Evan ground out, glaring at Christopher.

Patrick raised his eyebrows. "That's what you're so bent out of shape about? Get your mind on the fucking mission."

"Maybe you can put a tracking device on her. Then you'll know where she is at all hours," Brent said, egging him on. "Christopher can set you up."

"Go fuck yourself," Christopher said dryly, grabbing his gear. Christopher was the computer whiz of their SEAL team. He could hack into anything, find anyone. Although Evan had no doubt that he could indeed track anyone down, Brent was just being an ass.

Evan checked over his gear one last time, ensuring everything was in place before they got boots on the ground. Patrick's eyes landed on Evan, cool and assessing. Unless Rebecca and Ali had sat down for a little heart-to-heart after they'd flown out, and Rebecca had shared that info with Patrick, the man knew about as much as him.

Nothing.

***

They rolled to the edge of the small village in their convoy, bumping over the uneven dirt road. Evan spoke quietly into his mouthpiece, "Target located. Two hundred yards north. No civilians in sight."

"Roger that," drawled Matthew, trailing behind in a second vehicle.

The building was located near the perimeter of the cluster of small homes and crumbling buildings. It looked like next to nothing, a dilapidated structure left for nature to finish off. Their intel was one hundred percent accurate though, with hacked emails confirming the American was being held here. It was small, isolated, and out of the way. The soldier would be well-guarded. Tucked out of sight. And the enemy fuckers wouldn't have a chance.

Patrick gave the command, and Evan sped forward, coming to a stop right outside the enemy's walls. Four members of their SEAL team jumped out of the humvees and disappeared into the night, weapons locked and loaded, night-vision goggles on, tactical gear in place.

Evan gripped the steering wheel, clenching his teeth. It was so fucking quiet around here, something just didn't feel right. The SEAL team quickly scaled the walls and disappeared from his line of vision.

"Exterior guard taken out," Mike quietly spoke over their headsets. "Moving in."

Evan heard a rustle through his earpiece as the men burst through the doors of the building. "Two guards down," Patrick said. "Moving toward the stairs."

Long seconds ticked by as Evan scanned the area. Still too fucking quiet, even for the middle of the night.

"Room located," Brent said. "We're going in."

Another muffled sound, followed by gunshots came through the earpiece. Evan tensed and reached for his weapon. He was to remain in the vehicle, but if the shit hit the fan, he was going in after his men. Their guns all had silencers, which meant they'd engaged in enemy fire.

"Enemy down. Package acquired," Patrick said. "Grab him and go."

"The hostage needs medical attention," Mike said. "Call ahead to base. Rolling out in one minute."

"Roger that," Evan muttered. He pulled forward, looping around in a circle as he pointed the humvee back in the direction they'd come. The second the men jumped in, they were rolling out before someone came back and noticed the hostage was gone. Or that the front door had been busted open.

He released a breath he hadn't even realized he'd been holding. Thirty more seconds and those guys would be back over the wall.

He hit a small bump in the sandy ground, and the subsequent explosion was deafening. Red and orange flames lit up the night as his vehicle tumbled through the air, and Evan's head smashed into the side. The pain was excruciating as his neck snapped back. The humvee crashed to the ground, shaking his entire body around like a rag doll. He began to see stars and felt the heat of the blazing fire outside as dizziness overcame his body.

The last thing he saw was Alison's face in his mind before everything went black.

Chapter 19

Alison drummed her fingers on the table in the break room of the hospital. Something was wrong. Rebecca had called in a panic earlier from the courthouse, saying she'd gotten word that someone was injured. The fact that she hadn't spoken directly with Patrick had her sobbing into the phone. Alison's own heart had stopped at the idea of Evan being hurt. What if he was the one who'd sustained an injury so critical he'd been airlifted to some damn military hospital in Germany?

She'd tried to console her friend, tried not to even consider that Evan was the one hurt. But the idea that any man on Evan's SEAL team was injured had her chest tightening in worry. Her stomach heaving in nausea. Her heart breaking at the idea it could be Evan injured and never coming home.

Rebecca had mumbled something about a head injury and coma. She had no idea which of the men had been harmed.

Alison stood and paced the break room. She was antsy, restless as hell. She wanted nothing more than to run out the hospital doors to her car, jump in, and hightail it over to Evan's apartment. Except that he wasn't there.

Rebecca didn't even know where the men were. When they'd return. Some commander from Little Creek had gotten word to her that the other men were on a flight back to the States. When they'd left was anyone's guess. Alison's gut clenched. What if they weren't all returning?

If Evan was the man injured, she'd be on the next flight to Germany. She had leave saved up. She was a nurse. No one would stop her from being at his side for his entire recovery. Hell, she could even assist with his care. She sat down again, her hands shaking. The butterflies in her stomach were ridiculous. She didn't even know if he was the man hurt. All she needed was to hear his voice, and she'd be fine. Scratch that—all she needed was to know that he'd be okay. The relief coursing through her body at knowing he was here, safe, sound, and back in Virginia Beach was all she asked for.

If he didn't want to be with her after the way she'd flipped out on him, she'd understand. He just needed to be okay.

She glanced at her phone, willing it to ring. Rebecca would call her the second she heard anything. There was absolutely nothing she could do at the moment. How long was a flight back? She assumed the rest of the team was in the Middle East if the injured man had been sent to Germany. What the hell did she know though?

She briefly wondered if any of her colleagues at the hospital had contacts in Landstuhl. It wasn't unheard of—they could've gone to medical or nursing school together. Worked together at some point. But really, what was she going to do? Send out an email to the entire hospital staff asking if anyone knew someone there?

She was being ridiculous. Glancing at the clock, she saw she only had a few minutes left on her break. Five more hours on her shift, and she'd be that much closer to finding out where the guys were and who was hurt. If they weren't on their flight already when the commander called Rebecca, they must've flown out shortly after that.

She sighed.

It was going to be the longest afternoon of her life.

***

The headache pounding through Evan's skull was relentless. Never-ending. The aches filling his body made him feel about a hundred years old. It wasn't one thing that hurt. His entire body screamed for relief. So this was what it felt like to die.

"Flip, man, wake up," someone urged. Was that Patrick? Evan struggled to open his eyes. Why the hell was it so bright? They'd conducted this op in the middle of the night. The last thing he'd seen was the blast in the darkness.

A beeping sound to his left caught his attention. He turned his head slightly toward it but squeezed his eyes tighter. The lights and sounds were unbearable.

Someone pricked his arm with a needle. No, it was an IV. There were tubes and monitors all over him, he slowly realized. Seeing the nurse's scrubs as he opened his eyes, his heart rate accelerated. The pain momentarily subsided.

Oh.

Not Alison.

But he was in a hospital. He was alive. The meds they had him on made him loopy and tired. Confused. Where the hell was he? He tried to open his mouth to speak, but whatever medicine she'd added to his IV just now made it really hard to keep his eyes open. Maybe he'd just sleep for a few more minutes. Then everything would make sense. He was just so damn tired....

***

One more hour, and her shift would finally be over. Alison used to think the night shifts she pulled when she was younger were the longest hours of her life, but none of them topped this. She counted every second. Each minute felt like hours. It felt like days had passed since Rebecca called earlier. It was almost painful to glance at the clock and realize barely any time had elapsed.

She jumped as she was paged over the loudspeaker. Had Rebecca come to the ER to see her? Dear God, something must really be wrong.

She ran to the front desk of the emergency room and stopped short at the sight of Patrick in his camo. He was massive and intimidating. Completely out of place. Had he come straight here after he'd landed? Where was Rebecca?

Patrick was here, and Evan wasn't.

She ran to him, tears streaming down her cheeks.

Without a word, Patrick pulled her into an embrace, his large body holding her. He ducked his head down to her ear and spoke in a low, commanding tone. "Evan was injured, but he's stable. I'll take you to see him."

Alison looked up at him and nodded, tears running down her cheeks.

"Where is he?"

"Walter Reed, up in Maryland. We'll hop a military flight up to Andrew's. I'll be with you the entire time."

Two hours later, after the absolute longest flight and car ride of her life, they'd finally arrived at the military hospital. Patrick flashed his ID and seemed to know enough people to get her where she needed to go, stat. Between his camo and her scrubs, they fit right in anyway.

They wound through endless corridors of white halls, the beeping of machines and low voices coming from hospital rooms the only sounds. Her heart beat so fast, it nearly pounded right out of her chest. "I told Evan you were coming," Patrick murmured quietly as they walked. "He's gone through enough shock."

"Right," Alison said nervously, swallowing. Shit. What if he was mad at her?

Patrick eyed her, his blue eyes cool. "That man is in love with you, Alison."

She nodded, a tear slipping down her cheek. "I'm in love with him, too."

"I know."

A second later, and she was walking into his room. Evan was lying in a hospital bed, wearing an ugly blue gown, a white bandage wrapped around his head. His face looked battered and bruised, but his bright blue eyes flashed and a huge grin lit up his face as she stood nervously in the doorway. "Ali, thank God."

Relief washed through her, and she rushed over to him. She hovered over his bed, not wanting to hurt him, but Evan lifted her right off the floor and into his arms.

She collapsed on top of him, wrapping her arms around his broad chest, nestling close, as Patrick excused himself, closing the door. She burst into tears as Evan held her to him, and she cried and cried, inhaling his scent and savoring the feel of his warm body flush against her own. He was okay, and she was exactly where she belonged.

"It's okay, baby," he murmured, running his hand down her hair as his other arm tightened around her waist. "I've got you."

Epilogue

One month later

"You didn't have to drive all the way up to Walter Reed to get me," Evan said as they pulled into his apartment complex in Virginia Beach. "One of the guys could've driven me home."

"No way," Alison laughed. "You're mine, and I don't share."

Evan chuckled beside her. "Damn, woman, what's gotten into you?"

"Hopefully just you," she teased, her green eyes lighting with fire. She was feisty as hell today, teasing and flirting with him the entire drive back from Maryland. He wasn't sure what she was up to, but hell if he didn't love it. After a month in the hospital, he was desperate for some time alone with her. Evan's eyes flared, and he stretched across the front seat, capturing her lips in a searing kiss.

"Let's get you inside first," she chastised.

Heat coursed through him, and he quickly climbed out of Ali's car. After his week's stay in Landstuhl and month-long stint at Walter Reed, Evan was fully recovered and more than ready for life to return to normal. With Ali at his side and in his bed.

He opened the door to his apartment, his brows creasing as he looked around. A vase of flowers sat on the kitchen table, and he noticed a new package of coffee on the counter. Had Ali picked up that stuff? She smirked as he glanced around. Wandering through the apartment, he saw a stack of women's magazines on the coffee table. And was that a pile of Ali's clothes on top of his dresser? "I brought a few of my things, since I'll be over here so much."

"Is that so?" Evan asked, a smile breaking out over his face.

"Uh-huh. Most girlfriends leave some stuff at their boyfriend's apartments, right?"

"I guess," he teased, wandering into the bathroom. Her toothbrush sat on the counter right beside his. He looked back to see her face had fallen.

"I love your stuff, here," he murmured, walking across the room to her. "I'd just been planning to spend all my time at your nice, big townhouse instead." He bent down and kissed her softly.

"Oh," she breathed around his kisses. "That sounds perfect."

"Uh-huh," he teased, mimicking her. "But since we're already here, I plan to spend the entire night making love to you."

"It's only two in the afternoon," she giggled.

"Even better. We've got all day and all night," he

said huskily.

His hands slid to the hem of the dress she had on, and he tugged it up and over her head. Black lace covered her breasts, and the teeniest, tiniest black lace thong covered her mound. The high heels she'd slipped into when they'd walked into his apartment suddenly made a helluva lot more sense. Fucking gorgeous.

"Jesus, Ali," he breathed.

She grinned and walked over to his bed, her ass swinging back and forth. His groin tightened as he stared at her smooth, perfectly rounded bottom. All of Ali's panties had seemed sexy-as-hell, but that thong was insane. He was rock hard as he stalked after her toward the bed. She coyly looked over her shoulder at him, that long strawberry blonde hair cascading down her back, and she was like his every fantasy come to life. He stopped behind her, his large hands gripping her slender hips, and he pulled her toward him, grinding his erection into her ass.

"Fuck, baby. I like this side of you."

She turned her head, tilting it up toward him, and they kissed. Slowly. Sweetly. What started as a slow burn was quickly grower hotter, about to lead to an explosion. He'd never get enough of this woman. His hands rose to her breasts, kneading and caressing them through the lace. They swelled under his touch, and he plucked and pinched her pert little nipples as she whimpered and moaned.

"Evan," she breathed.

"I know I said I was planning to spend time at your place, but with you looking like this, I may never let you leave."

Alison laughed then gasped as his hand slid down

to cup her sex. She was his, and Evan was about to show her just how badly he wanted—needed— her. He could feel her bare lips through the lace, and it was the sexiest damn thing in the world. She was already wet, dripping for him. He'd planned to take his time exploring her body, getting reacquainted with the curves he'd dreamed about in the hospital, but he was so hard and she was so ready, he needed to be inside her this instant.

Ali seemed to know exactly what effect her skimpy little lingerie would have on him. It was hotter than hell to know she'd dressed this morning just for him. "How much do you like these panties?" he growled.

"What?" she gasped as he massaged her sex through the lace.

"I'm going to rip them off."

She whimpered, and he yanked the scrap of fabric away. "I'll buy you all the sexy lingerie you want," he ground out. "Tomorrow. Climb up on the bed."

She complied, edging up on her hands and knees, still wearing those sexy heels. Fuck. He rested his large hand at the center of her back, gently pushing her down until her ass was up in the air. He grabbed a condom from his nightstand, quickly unfastening his pants and sheathing himself. His pants slid to his knees, and he didn't give a fuck. He stepped to the edge of the bed and rubbed his throbbing cock through her wet folds.

"Evan," she moaned.

He toyed with her a moment, letting his thick length brush up against her clit. She gasped.

Ali looked like a seductress sent down from heaven in nothing but those come-fuck-me heels and black lace bra. He could feel her wet heat as his cock nudged at her entrance, and a moment later, he was slowly edging inside her molten core. She clamped down around him immediately, moaning his name like she needed him more than anything else in the world.

***

Alison moaned as Evan's thick length slowly penetrated her. He stretched and filled her, letting her know she belonged only to him. Her hair cascaded around her, blanketing her view, tickling her shoulders, and she felt bare and exposed bent before Evan this way. His large hands gripped her hips as he held her—not too tightly, but in a way that let her know he was in complete and utter control. She felt like some kind of sex goddess wearing nothing but sky-high heels and black lace. No man ever made her feel this way before. Evan brought out a side in her that made her feel cherished and cared for yet desired and worshipped all at the same time.

She wanted everything in Evan—a friend, a lover, an entire lifetime together.

He bottomed out, filling her more deeply than he'd ever been before. It was erotic and sexy as hell having a man take her from behind this way. He dominated her, controlled every movement—and she freaking loved the power he currently had over her. He gently began to thrust into her, and she moaned. Evan was in complete control of their lovemaking, his thick erection stroking her inner walls. Claiming her. She gently thrust back against him, meeting him stroke for stroke.

White light flashed before her eyes. Her sex

gripped him tighter, and she softly cried out.

He groaned in approval, murmuring quietly to her. "You're mine, Ali. Say that you're mine."

"Yes," she gasped, shockwaves of pleasure bursting right through her. Evan's hand slid down to her clit, softly caressing her, and she screamed, her orgasm coming from nowhere. She bucked wildly back against him, Evan carrying her through the intense ways of pleasure. Rather than climaxing himself, Evan pulled out and flipped her over. She gazed up at him, shocked to see the tenderness in his eyes after that erotic encounter. Muscular arms wrapped around her, and he moved her to the center of the bed, his cock twitching.

"Leave the shoes on," he said with a grin.

She smiled, flushing, and he gripped her knees, spreading her legs wide open for him. The next instant, Evan was prowling over her body, his weight settling on top of her. His erection nudged at her center, and he slowly entered her again. Her walls still spasmed around him, the aftershocks from her orgasm rippling through her body. Her sex milked him, making Evan groan. He kissed her, his manhood nestled deep inside her core, and made love to her slowly.

Pressure began to build once again inside of her, and she clutched onto his shoulders, desperately needing to hang on. His blue eyes bore into hers. "You're mine, Ali."

"And you're mine."

His tongue dipped into her mouth, ending further conversation. He rocked into her harder, faster, and she wrapped her legs around his waist, her heels digging into his ass. Evan shifted positions, somehow stroking her even deeper inside. His large hand slid between them, down to her bare sex, and he stroked her clit with his thumb. Fireworks began to explode in her mind, the sensation nearly too much to bear.

He thrust again and again, filling her, claiming her, and as his thumb circled her clit again, she screamed. His mouth muffled her cries, and she clung to him, her anchor in the midst of her fall. She was drowning, lost to everything but this man.

Evan inside of her was pure heaven.

Minutes later, she lay wrapped in Evan's strong embrace. His arms were wrapped possessively around her, holding her close. Keeping her safe. His fingertips softly caressed her arm, and he buried his face in her hair.

"Are you okay?" she asked as he pulled her tightly against his chest.

"I'm perfect," he said, planting a kiss on her bare shoulder.

She twisted in his arms to face him, and Evan's eyes shone brighter than she'd ever seen. He lifted one of her legs up over his hip, their sexes rubbing together, and she could feel Evan already growing hard again. For her.

"I love you, Ali."

"I love you, too."

He dipped his head toward her, kissing her gently.

"But I don't want us going back and forth between your place and mine," she said, a smile playing on her lips.

"You don't?" His lips quirked as he watched her.

"I was thinking maybe you should just move in with me."

"You were, huh?" he asked. Mischief sparkled in

his blue eyes.

"Well, you'll have to grill for me. And make me dinner," she teased.

"I do make killer spaghetti," he joked. "Anything else?" he asked, lightly tracing her lips with his fingertip.

"You have to make love to me like that every night."

"Done." He bent forward and kissed her again.

"Promise?" she teased.

"Yep. Sealed with a kiss."

Evan rolled onto his back, pulling her along, too, so that she straddled him. The grin on his face lit up her entire world. Having this powerful man beneath her, in love with her, was more than she'd ever dreamed about.

Evan was hers.

Forever.

Author's Note

Thanks for picking up book two in my Alpha SEALs series! Evan and Ali were an easy couple to pair up—some characters just go together. She thought from the beginning that Evan was too young for her and was reluctant to give the youngest guy on the team a chance, but his easygoing ways were just what she needed to get over her fears and past hurt. And the sparks between them! Whew! **Fans Self**

Every SEAL on the team will be getting his own book, so make sure to check out Christopher's story next. Who is the mystery woman he's had on his mind for all these years?

Stop by my Facebook page and say hi for teasers and excerpts of my upcoming releases. I always love to hear from my readers and welcome any feedback.

xoxo,
Makenna

About the Author

Makenna Jameison is a bestselling romance author. She writes military romance and romantic suspense with hot alpha males, steamy scenes, and happily-ever-afters. Her debut series made it to #1 in Romance Short Stories on Amazon.

Makenna loves the beach, strong coffee, red wine, and traveling. She lives in Washington DC with her husband and two daughters.

Visit www.makennajameison.com to discover your next great read.

Want to read more from MAKENNA JAMEISON?

Keep reading for an exclusive excerpt from the third book in her Alpha SEALs series, *A SEAL's SURRENDER*.

Lexi Mattingly, a hotshot Pentagon security specialist, can't escape her past. Sent down to Little Creek to track down hackers attempting to infiltrate Top Secret naval databases, the last man she expects to run into is the ruggedly handsome Navy SEAL she left in Coronado a lifetime ago.

Navy SEAL Christopher "Blade" Walters has carried a torch for a decade. The sparks ignited years ago on the beaches of California never burned out, and the man destined to be alone feels them slowly combust when the woman he'd lost forever walks back into his life.

Lexi and Christopher must learn to work together to stop the hackers. But when she's kidnapped from her hotel, Christopher may be the only man who can save her. Can she trust the man who broke her heart to protect her life? And more importantly, can he convince her to give their love a second chance?

Chapter 1

Lexi Mattingly flipped her sleek, jet black hair over her shoulder and strode through the parking lot, her sky-high heels clicking as she walked across the black asphalt. The sweltering heat hit her like a sauna, the salty air that was blowing in from the ocean the only thing making it somewhat tolerable. She slipped off her suit jacket, walking the remaining few steps to her SUV in only her slim skirt and camisole.

The vast spread of buildings around Naval Amphibious Base Little Creek was nothing like the impenetrable rings of corridors at the Pentagon, her home turf. The only thing vaguely familiar was the sounds of planes in the air—although the fighter jets screaming across the sky on training drills from Oceana Naval Air Station in Virginia Beach weren't exactly the same as the commercial flights taking off from Reagan National Airport along the Potomac

River in Arlington.

She watched two FA-18 Hornets blaze across the blue sky, the image reminding her of a lifetime ago in Coronado. It was hard to believe nearly ten years had gone by since her days as a college student back in California. She'd built her career in Washington, DC, her drive to succeed and work ethic fitting in perfectly with the fast-paced, challenging lifestyle of the Department of Defense.

An IT whiz at the Pentagon, amongst the Defense Department's best-of-the-best, Lexi was called down to Little Creek to determine who was attempting to hack into the Top Secret databases at the naval base. Black Ops, names and identities of SEAL teams, mission specs, locations of forward-operating bases around the world—the intelligence stored there would be a wealth of information to foreign operatives. It would fetch a high price on the black market and make the US vulnerable to foreign adversaries. Lexi was tasked to ensure that the data never fell into the wrong hands. And to determine the source of the attempted infiltrations.

After spending the afternoon briefing the top brass at Little Creek about the vulnerabilities of their computer systems, she was ready to call it a day. Four hours of bumper-to-bumper traffic on I-95 and I-64 as she drove down from Arlington this morning followed by four hours spent in a cramped conference room on base, and she needed a drink. Preferably a stiff one.

She slung her suit jacket over one arm and clicked the remote to unlock her vehicle. The *chirp, chirp* resounded across the pavement. She certainly didn't need to set the alarm while on base, but old habits died hard.

A uniformed Navy officer eyed her appreciatively as he climbed out of his own car a few spaces over, but he merely nodded with a polite, "Ma'am."

She nodded back in acknowledgement and then smirked as she turned away. All the military men were so formal on base, under the watchful eyes of their supervisors and commanding officers. Get them in a bar after hours, a few drinks in, and they'd be hitting on her left and right. Insisting she needed to come home with them for the night.

Right.

She could also use a month-long vacation to a tropical island, but the chance of either of those things happening was zilch.

She hadn't minded the attention of handsome military men in the least in her college days. Back in California, hunky guys, hot beaches, and alcohol-fueled nights had filled her early twenties. Her first and only serious boyfriend, a ruggedly handsome Navy SEAL, had kept her up night after night, and she'd been more than happy to lose sleep basking in his attention. To let his years of experience guide her first sexual encounters. They were young, carefree, and had the world at their disposal.

Those days were long over now.

At twenty-nine, she'd spent the past seven years working her way up the ranks at the Department of Defense. She had an undergraduate degree in Computer Science, a Master's Degree from Georgetown that she'd completed while working full time—and she was good at what she did. Really good. An expert hacker and IT Security Specialist for the

Pentagon. Her expertise and vast knowledge was renowned, sought after by others in the military trying to lure her away to their Top Secret projects. Job offers flew in from defense contractors around the Beltway. But she'd found her home.

She enjoyed life at the Pentagon, the headquarters and central hub of activity for the DoD. She was tasked to assist the branches of the armed services on network security issues, so she'd come down to Little Creek for the week, first to brief the higher-ups and then to get down in the dirt and play with the big boys. Figuratively speaking, of course. Although she'd work side-by-side with their IT specialists and network security administrators in rooting out the source of the attempted hacks, no way in hell was she falling into bed with any of them. No matter how attractive a man in uniform may be.

Lexi climbed into her SUV, dropping her briefcase and blazer onto the passenger seat. She adjusted her skirt as she started the engine, feeling the ache in her calves from walking around base in those damn heels all afternoon. Nothing sounded better right now than changing into some comfortable clothes and grabbing a drink at a bar down by the water.

She grabbed her buzzing cell phone from her briefcase, her best friend Kenley's picture flashing across the screen.

"Hi hun. Did you get my message?" she asked as she cranked up the AC. She pictured Kenley, petite with cascading brown curls, anxiously pacing back and forth in front of their favorite bar back in DC. The same place they were supposed to meet for drinks tonight before the game.

"Yeah, I just got it—I was stuck in meetings all

day. You're down there all week?" Kenley moaned. "Who's going to come to the Nat's game with me tonight?"

Lexi laughed. "I'm sure you'll find some poor guy to drag along."

"Two hours before the first pitch?"

"Call Cassidy," she said, referring to the third woman in their trio of friends. Tall and blonde, she was the exact opposite in looks from Lexi and Kenley, but the three of them had met just after college and were inseparable.

"No, she's tied up with what's-his-name."

"Literally?" Lexi asked with a chuckle. It was only five o'clock on a Monday night, but then again, you never knew with Cassidy.

"God, I hope not. TMI."

A smile played on Lexi's lips. If walls could talk, the ones in Cassidy's apartment would have enough stories to last a lifetime. "Sorry about the change in plans for tonight. I wasn't expecting to be sent down here—"

"But you're the best," Kenley finished with a sigh. "Can't I convince you to move over to the private sector? I could find you a kick-ass job. You'd pick your hours, decide which business trips you want—"

"Not a chance," Lexi laughed.

This must've been the twentieth time Kenley had pitched Lexi into abandoning the DoD for work at a large defense contractor. Although it might be fun working with her best friend, her career and interests were with the government. Fat chance she'd abandon that now after the years she'd put in, no matter how big the paycheck. With a few side IT projects that she was able to moonlight on—legally—she didn't really need the extra cash anyway.

"It was worth a shot," Kenley mumbled. "Oh great, and now there's a creepy old guy checking me out. I should not be standing here alone in front of a bar."

"How old?"

"I don't know. Fifty. Too old. Ugh. All right, I'll head in and grab a drink myself. I feel like I'm on display out here."

"Tell him you have an extra ticket to the game," Lexi teased. "Maybe he could be your sugar daddy."

"Not a chance in hell. I'm so calling you back though if that creeper starts hitting on me."

"That's what best friends are for."

The two women hung up, and Lexi pulled out of the parking lot on base. She nodded at the guards as she exited. Damn, even they were good-looking. By Friday, she hoped to have this project wrapped up and be headed back to Northern Virginia. She was an expert at tracking down hackers and installing top-notch security systems impenetrable by anyone. If the hackers were in the US—doubtful—they'd be arrested. If they were on foreign soil, she'd see to it that they never made it past the firewalls and security systems she'd install at Little Creek. And maybe she'd give them a taste of their own medicine. A few lines of seemingly innocuous code, and their systems would be fried.

The day spent on base might've been perfect if it weren't for those damn SEALs all over the place. The men stationed at Little Creek reminded her a little too much of her former flame. She'd moved clear across the damn country to avoid seeing him again, abandoning her work at Coronado for life at the

Pentagon. Not that her asshole of an ex had ever tried to track her down—he was scared senseless of commitment, of raising a family, of doing the right thing. And didn't that say a lot about the man—no, make that *boy*—that he was. He'd been young at the time, too, but any decent guy would've manned up. Taken responsibilities for his actions.

A pregnancy scare when she was twenty, after they'd been dating for a couple years, had shown his true colors. He wasn't the settling down type. Not the marrying kind. Certainly not fit to be a father. Maybe the false alarm had been for the best—she'd seen firsthand he wasn't the type of man to ever be happy about starting a family together, so she'd left. It might've broken her heart if she didn't hate him so damn much.

She'd hauled her ass across the country to avoid ever seeing him again. How's that for a reasonable reaction? God, if her parents had ever known the real reason she'd left California, they'd have a field day. He was never good enough, smart enough for her. She hadn't given a crap, but look where she'd ended up today. Single and alone at age twenty-nine.

Life at the Pentagon was good, but she missed the sea and warm weather. Washington just wasn't the same as laid-back California, and there were days when her homesickness hit her like a tidal wave, knocking her breathless. Maybe she'd look into transferring to a naval base here in Virginia one day. With seven years spent working her way up in the Department of Defense, she wasn't ready to jump ship. She'd stay with the DoD and still get to enjoy life near the water. She'd miss her friends and the life she'd built, but maybe a small part of her soul would finally feel at peace. Maybe.

One thing was for certain—she'd never, ever set foot in Coronado again.

Six feet of solid muscle, warm brown eyes, and the hottest sex she'd ever had in her life had left her smitten with her first love. He was hotter than sin, a SEAL barely out of BUD/S when they'd first crossed paths. He'd taken her virginity, captured her heart, and promised her the world. Life had been pretty damn perfect until she'd thought she was pregnant. No question it was his. She'd never so much as let another man undress her before, let alone make love to her night after night.

The cold way he'd frozen up and questioned her loyalty to him made her want to rip his heart right out. To pound her fists against his chest until he apologized. To hurt him the cruel way he'd hurt her. He'd attempted to ask for her forgiveness the next day, but it was too late. That ship had sailed, and she sure as hell didn't plan to ever speak to him again. She'd moved a week later, never once looking back on the life that could've been. The future she should've had. She didn't even know what the hell had happened to him. It's not like the movements and career of a SEAL were broadcast on the national news. And he sure as hell hadn't tried to follow her, contact her, or do a damn thing to win her back.

It was better this way. She had her busy career, her friends, and her condo in Arlington. An occasional date, but never anything serious. She certainly didn't need a man to come into her life and break her heart again. The SEALs at Little Creek had sent too many thoughts swirling around her mind—memories she couldn't forget, some memories she didn't want to forget. And one memory that chased her all these years later—of chocolate brown eyes that saw into her very soul. Then betrayed her when she needed him the most.

Now Available in Paperback!

Made in the USA
Columbia, SC
08 August 2021

43210010R00121